ESCAPE TO THE GUNFLINT

By the Same Author

How to Overcome A Bad Back
Stop Procrastinating—DO IT!
Rejection

ESCAPE to the GUNFLINT

JAMES R. SHERMAN

Pathway Books 👣
700 Parkview Terrace
Golden Valley, Minnesota 55416
(612) 377-1521

Library of Congress Catalog Number
82-82206

International Standard Book Number
0-935538-04-6

Illustrations by Arlen Olson

Pathway Books
700 Parkview Terrace
Golden Valley, Minnesota 55416
(612) 377-1521

For my mom and dad who introduced
me to the Gunflint Trail.

PUBLISHER'S NOTE

⟪FRIDAY

"That rotten, little fink! He's done it again!"

Dick Christopher was furious. The forty-two year old computer architect had just discovered while reading his company's newsletter that another of his design concepts had been pirated. His divisional vice-president had underhandedly taken credit for a new, integrated-memory system that Dick had been working on for months.

This wasn't the first time that Cyrus Bransky had stolen one of Dick's ideas. But it took Dick until recently to discover what could happen if it were allowed to continue. Dick's salary, and possible promotions, were based on his ability to come up with new ideas. If he didn't get credit for the work he did, he could lose his job.

The company Dick worked for designed and manufactured desktop computers. It was one of the most progressive and successful firms in Minneapolis, and it was headed by an ex-naval officer who believed results were the best indicators of an employee's success. The Captain didn't usually care *how* the results were achieved, he just wanted to make sure the company continued to grow and prosper.

The Captain saw to it that the performance-based salaries were excellent, but ethical standards were sometimes ignored. The administrative staff members were expected to discipline themselves through an honor system. If a problem came up, the people involved were expected to work it out by themselves. The Captain would only get involved when something happened to jeopardize the operation of the company.

The people who worked there were generally good people. But sometimes the stress of the marketplace caused them to do things they wouldn't normally do. On the other hand, it was not unusual for Cyrus

1

Bransky to be involved in situations that involved ethical issues. Dick looked at the article again. Next to Bransky's picture was a lengthy explanation of how the system had been developed. Dick knew what the article said without reading it. It was a complete breakdown of everything he'd done for the past eighteen months, but his name wasn't mentioned anywhere.

Dick's anger continued to build as he thought about Bransky and what he'd done. He could hardly believe that his division chief would continue to steal other people's ideas. But then, after he thought about it, he figured Bransky was capable of doing just about anything.

Cyrus Bransky was one of the first people the Captain hired. He thought Cyrus had a combat record, but actually, Cyrus had spent eight years as an Air Force mechanic at a base in Arizona. Cyrus had barely gotten through high school and resented anyone else who had gone on for additional education.

Cyrus was short, partially bald, and a little on the heavy side. His success came in bullying people and in capitalizing on other people's accomplishments. The Captain didn't particularly like Cyrus, but he kept him on because he felt he owed him something. Cyrus had helped the company get through some very difficult times when they were first starting, and the Captain appreciated that. Now, however, Cyrus kept his position as Vice-President by fighting anyone who tried to take it away from him. He probably pirated Dick's idea because he thought he could impress the Captain.

Regardless of the reason behind it, Dick had seen enough of it. This time, he thought he could take on Bransky in a fight for recognition and win. He'd kept careful records of the time he'd spent, the alternatives he'd considered, and the people he'd talked to. Now he felt it was time to stand up for what he thought was right.

Dick kicked his metal wastebasket and sent it crashing against the wall. Then he stormed out of his office, slammed the door, and headed for Bransky's office on the other side of the company complex.

The people in his area didn't look up when he went through, but Dick could see them smiling. He thought they'd already read the newsletter and probably knew where he was going. Some of them were obviously excited about the prospect of a fight, just like a playground full of kids.

Dick moved quickly through the elevated walkway that led to the administrative building. When he entered the outer lobby, the young receptionist at the desk tried to stop him as he headed for the executive wing. He ignored her and continued to the suite of inner offices. Becky Richards was waiting for him as he approached Bransky's door. She'd worked in Dick's area before being promoted to division secretary, and the two of them were still very good friends. As Dick walked by, she smiled and looked aside, pretending she didn't see him. Dick charged right into Bransky's office without knocking and found Cyrus sitting at his desk, clipping his fingernails.

"What do you want?" demanded Cyrus as he jumped to his feet. But before Dick could answer, Cyrus turned toward the door and yelled at Becky. "Did you let him in here? I told you..."

"Sit down, Bransky," said Dick.

"You can get into a lot of trouble talking to me like that," said Cyrus. "As a matter of fact, you're already in a lot of trouble for busting in here the way you did. I could..."

"What are you trying to pull, Bransky? I saw the newsletter this morning with the article saying *you'd* developed the new, integrated-memory system. You know that was my project. You had nothing to do with it."

"It was developed in my division," said Cyrus, "and I'm responsible for everything that comes out of here. Besides, you only had an idea. I improved it so it'd work."

"Bransky, I can't believe how dumb you really are. I've got extensive drawings of every aspect of that project, and they're all dated and signed by Security. I've also got tapes of you and me talking about the project through every stage of development. They're also dated. So there's no way you could get credit for doing anything on that project.

"I've had it with you, Bransky. You've screwed me before, but you're not going to do it again. This time I've covered my tracks. And when I go to the Captain with the stuff I've got, your name is going to be mud."

"You've made a big mistake, Christopher, charging in here like this."

"You made the mistake, Bransky. And I'm going to see that you hang for it."

"Wait a minute, smart ass. You forget that I've got a lot of clout in this organization. I wouldn't be in this position if I didn't. So if you try to get cute with me, I'll see to it that you get your butt kicked out of here so fast it'll make your head swim. You'll get nothing out of it either; no severance, no profit sharing, nothing. And I can do it, because I'm good at it."

Dick was surprised at Bransky's sudden aggressiveness and his attempts to gain control of the situation. But he was ready for him.

"Come off it, Bransky. After the Captain sees what I've got, you're going to be the one who gets kicked out of here."

"I'll fight you, Christopher, and I won't lose."

"Well stayed tuned, Buckwheat. We'll see who gets the axe."

Dick turned around and stormed out of Bransky's office, slamming the door behind him. Becky blew him a kiss as he went by, and he gave her a wink in return.

The young receptionist tried again to stop Dick as he went through the lobby, but he ignored her and continued toward the elevated walkway. As he opened the outer door, he thought someone was following him. He turned and saw Matt Weed walking toward him.

Matt was Vice President for Financial Affairs. He'd been with the company since it started and knew it from top to bottom, but he seldom got away from his books and numbers. Dick liked Matt even though they hadn't spent much time together.

"Dick," said Matt, "that was quite a run-in you just had with Cyrus Bransky. What are you going to do about it?"

"I don't know yet," said Dick. "I've got enough to hang him out to dry if the Captain would go along with me."

"I doubt it," said Matt. "Cyrus got where he is by chewing up people like you. You're probably dealing with a short deck. He'll fight hard and challenge everything you throw at him."

Dick suddenly felt demoralized. The emotional high he built up during his altercation with Bransky was quickly turning into a low.

"Hey, don't give up," said Matt as he saw the change in Dick's expression. "I just think you've got a much bigger fight on your hands than you realize. I've known Cyrus a lot longer than you have, and I know what kind of person he is. He's not very smart, but he's ruthless as hell. He'll stop at nothing to get his own way. If you get him backed into a corner, he'll go crazy. He's done some unbelievable things around here when others have taken him on, and he's gotten away with it. I'm not afraid of him, but I'd hate to think of what he would do if I ever crossed him. So if you're going after him, you'd better have more amunition than you have now, or he'll eat you alive."

"What you you mean?" asked Dick.

"You need something to strengthen your position, like falsified financial records, or evidence of payoffs and skimming. Bransky is into all of it, and I can give you what you need to nail him. But there's a risk involved. The company image could suffer if you and Bransky got into an all-out fight. It might cause us to lose some important contracts that are coming up. If that happens, the Captain will move in. He'll make sure the fight is between the two of you, and he'll see to it that nobody else gets involved. If it's a bad fight, both of you could lose your jobs and end up on the outside.

"I don't think you're going to be able to work with Cyrus anymore after what just happened. But you've still got several other options. You can quit without a fight, give your stuff to the Captain, and come out smelling like a rose. Your profit sharing and pension rights are vested, so if you go out graciously, you won't lose a thing. But if you fight Cyrus and lose, you'll probably get tossed out of the company and lose a lot of money in the process. Of course if you fight Cyrus and win, we all get rid of a real bastard, and you're in like Flynn. The Captain is the key. If he doesn't want a fight right now, then it's all over."

"What do you think I ought to do?" asked Dick.

"You're going to have to do this on your own," said Matt. "I'll give you all the data I can, but you'll have to put it together. I can't get anymore involved than that. I just don't have the stomach for it. My ulcer would explode if I so much as lifted a finger in your behalf."

"Well I'm ready to take him on right now," said Dick.

"You don't have to commit yourself right now," said Matt. "Take some time and make sure of what you're going to do. You can still chip away at Cyrus while you're deciding. Drop some hints. Give him something to worry about. There's an outside chance you could get the upper hand right away. Tell him you're writing a critique of the Atchison contract. He'll probably wet his pants on that one."

"What about the Atchison contract?"

"Cyrus skimmed a lot off the top of that one," said Matt. "The Captain allowed him to make some payoffs if he had to, but Cyrus went beyond that. He not only pocketed the Captain's money, but he also pulled in some cash from some of our suppliers. So he got it from both ends. I can fill you in on the details after you've decided what you're going to do."

"I really appreciate this, Matt. How can I thank you?"

"Don't worry about it," said Matt. "I'd really like to help you, because we need men like you in the company. And it wouldn't hurt to get rid of a bastard like Cyrus. Now I've got to get back to my office. Take the weekend to think about what you're going to do. Or take longer if you have to. Just give me a call when you've made up your mind. I'll do what I can to help as long as I can stay on the sidelines."

Dick shook hands with Matt and watched him go back to his office. Suddenly, the situation had gotten a lot more complicated than it was an hour ago. Dick needed some time to think, so instead of going directly to his office, he went down to the lower level and out the back door to the parking lot. No one was on the jogging and hiking path, so he decided to go for a walk and try to sort everything out.

It was very hard for Dick to deal with Cyrus Bransky because of their lousy relationship. He knew there would be other confrontations just like there had been in the past, and he'd give anything to be able to avoid them.

Dick knew the information Matt had was really not a part of the memory-system fiasco, but it might get Bransky fired if he brought it in with his own documentation. That, however, would take a lot of analysis and preparation, and he already had lots of material to sort through before he took his case to the Captain. So even if he could strengthen his position by using Matt's data, the effort in doing so might be more than he could handle.

Then Dick thought about the Captain. He was the key, just like Matt said. As head of the company, he still called most of the shots. So Dick knew he'd better understand where the Captain stood before he opened fire on Bransky.

Dick had seen the Captain operate in a situation like this about two years ago when the production and marketing people got into a big hassle. The Captain kept the fight contained and stepped in only when an outside conflict had to be resolved. It was a bloody fight, and both division chiefs ended up leaving the company. Dick knew for sure that he didn't want to go through the same kind of fight with Bransky.

As Dick walked across the company complex, he tried to sort out all the options that were open to him. Four of them seemed to stand out.

First of all, he could stay in the company and fight Bransky for what he thought was right. Or he could stay and do nothing, hoping that things would straighten out over time. He could also quit his job and take a shot at Bransky from outside the company. Or he could quit and do nothing about Bransky or anything else that had gone on.

He still couldn't decide which option was best for him. The more things he considered, the more confused he got. There obviously were no easy solutions. After twenty minutes of muddling around, Dick went back to his office.

No one said anything to him as he came through the design area, but he could see that many of them were still smiling. He thought they probably already knew as much as he did about his encounter with Bransky.

Bill Douglas was waiting in Dick's office.

"You never were worth a damn at kicking field goals," said Bill. He held up Dick's dented wastebasket and the remains of a walnut picture frame that fell to the floor in his office.

"I'm sorry, Bill, but that son of a bitch really got to me."

"So what are you going to do about it?"

"I don't know yet," said Dick. "I'd like to hammer him into the floor, but it's a lot more complicated than that." Until Dick knew what he was going to do, he thought he'd better keep Matt's information confidential. Bill was a good friend and a top man to work with, but Dick felt he needed to work his problem out alone, at least for the time being.

"What's so complicated?" asked Bill. "He pirated another one of your design concepts, so kill him. It'd be justifiable homicide. I'd even do it for you if you'd take the blame."

"Thanks a lot," said Dick. "It's nice to have friends like you who are willing to stick their necks out. Seriously Bill, I've really got to think this through before I make a decision. I'd have to give up a lot if I fought

Bransky and lost. And even if I beat him the Captain could still decide to toss me out. I might just chuck the whole mess and walk off into the sunset."

"Do you mean quit?"

"Yes, and that wouldn't be so bad. I could always get another job. All my benefits are vested, so I'd be in reasonably good financial condition. Then I could move up north and run a bait and tackle shop on Lake Mille Lacs."

"Bullroar!" said Bill. "You're a fighter, not a quitter. Go after the son of a bitch."

"That's easy for you to say. It's not your head that's on the block."

"But you can't let him dump on you like this," said Bill. "The man is a menace."

"I know that. But the whole thing is a lot more complicated than I first thought. There are lots of variables to consider, and I need to get away and sort them all out."

"Why not go up north, find an island in the middle of a lake, and stake yourself to an anthill. Maybe you'll get a frigging vision."

"You know," said Dick, "that's a good idea. The anthill doesn't sound very good, but going up north sure does. I could take a week of annual leave and go up to the Gunflint Trail. A week in the wilderness would help me get a better perspective on the whole mess."

"Then do it," said Bill. "We can sure get along without you here."

Dick reached for the intercom and called Becky Richards.

"Becky? This is Dick."

"Well hello, tiger. What can I do for you?"

"Be a doll and sign me out for a week of annual leave, starting next Monday. I'll be back here the following Monday."

"What for," asked Becky, "round two?"

"Maybe so," said Dick, "but for now I just need to get away for a while."

"Okay, I'll do it. But only if you'll take me with you."

"You don't even know where I'm going."

"I don't care. Just take me away from here...Oh! Oh! The dragon just buzzed. I'd better see what your friend Bransky wants."

"Wait, Becky. Before I go, I want you to tell Bransky that I'll be working on a critique of the Atchison contract."

"You're what?"

"Just tell him. He'll understand."

Dick hung up the phone and started to laugh.

"What's that all about?" asked Bill.

"Just an inside joke," said Dick. "Listen, the division is moving along fine. There's nothing that can't be handled while I'm gone. So I think I'll take off first thing in the morning, stay up on the Gunflint Trail all next week, and come back a week from Monday. By then I'll have decided whether I'm going to fight Bransky or cut and run."

"Well good luck, my friend," said Bill. "I hope you can get something accomplished up there. On the other hand, it might be better if you stayed here and tried to work it through."

"I doubt it," said Dick. "There are too many distractions down here. As soon as I can get to the wilderness country, I'll be able to sort things out and come up with some answers. I just need to be by myself for a while."

Bill said goodbye and went back to his office. Then Dick gathered up the material he'd accumulated while he was working on the integrated-memory project. He didn't want to leave any of it for Bransky to find, and he knew he'd have to study it again before he went in to see the Captain.

It was almost noon when he went down the backstairs to the parking lot, got into his Volvo station wagon, and drove to his condominium. He had little more than a week to come up with a plan of action for dealing with Bransky, and he was anxious to get started. At the same time, he was experiencing a strange sense of apprehension. He pretty well knew what to expect from Bransky. But there was something beyond that, something he couldn't identify. He felt afraid, and he didn't know why. He tried to shake the feeling, but it stayed with him all the way home. Then it disappeared as mysteriously as it had come.

Cyrus Bransky was in a foul mood. He didn't like the way Christopher had come barging into his office, and now his secretary was not responding to his call on the intercom. When she finally did answer, he yelled at her.

"Where the hell have you been?"

"I'm sorry, Mr. Bransky. I was taking another call. Mr. Christopher left a message for you."

"Christopher? What did he want?"

"He said he was taking a few days off and wouldn't be back in the office until a week from Monday. He also said to tell you he was working on a critique of the Atchison contract."

Cyrus was stunned. Just the mention of that contract made his heart beat faster. He couldn't understand why Christopher would be meddling with the Atchison contract unless he knew something about the payoffs that were involved.

"Mr. Bransky?" asked Becky.

"What do you want?"

"Well you buzzed me, sir. What do you want?"

"I don't want anything," yelled Cyrus. "Just don't bother me. And hold all my calls until I get back to you." Cyrus slammed the receiver back on the phone.

"Old fart!" said Becky as she slammed down her phone.

Cyrus suddenly realized that Dick Christopher knew an awful lot about what was going on in the company. Either that or he was bluffing. Cyrus thought Christopher's complaints about pirating were insignificant. He was more concerned about his knowledge of the Atchison contract. Christopher must know something about the payoffs and skimming, but Cyrus couldn't understand why he hadn't mentioned it when he was in the office.

Christopher's threat to take everything to the Captain also bothered Cyrus. If Christopher had lots of facts and figures, and if the Captain bought his story, Cyrus could lose his job. On the other hand, if Christopher went in with unsubstantiated charges and lots of hearsay, the Captain would probably label him a troublemaker and end up firing him. Cyrus knew that Christopher wouldn't reveal his information until he saw the Captain. And whatever it was, Cyrus knew it could cause a lot of trouble.

Cyrus was not afraid of a fight. There had been others in the company who'd taken him on and lost. If Christopher was dumb enough to try it, he'd end up like the others did: out of a job. Cyrus knew that as long as he kept the Captain out of it, he could probably get away with murder.

Cyrus' thoughts were suddenly interrupted by the buzzing of his intercom.

"I told you I didn't want any calls," he yelled at Becky.

"It's Mr. Abernathy. He wants to talk to you on line one."

Timothy Abernathy had been hired a year ago by the Captain to be his executive assistant. Cyrus thought he was a real jerk. He was clearly the Captain's man, however, and Cyrus knew he had to talk to him. He punched the phone line without responding to Becky.

"This is Bransky."

"How are you this morning, Cyrus?"

Timothy Abernathy called everyone by their first name, but he expected everyone else to call him *Mr.* Abernathy. He was a cocky, thirty-year old bachelor with an M.B.A. degree from Northwestern University. He was always arrogant, often rude, and sometimes difficult to deal with. But he was also very close to the Captain. He came from a wealthy family that owned a lot of stock in the company and had been hired by the Captain as a favor to his father. After seeing him in action, the Captain got to like him. Almost everyone else in the company, including Cyrus, hated his guts.

"I'm fine, Mr. Abernathy," said Cyrus as he gritted his teeth. "How are you?"

"I'm fine too, Cyrus, but the Captain is somewhat distressed. He heard that you and Dick Christopher had a major disagreement this morning."

Cyrus cursed the company grapevine. The incident had happened less than an hour ago and already the Captain knew about it. "It's okay," he said.

"Oh, but it's not okay, Cyrus," said Abernathy. "It seems to be a major topic of conversation throughout the company. The Captain is afraid that if it isn't resolved soon, it might cause quite a bit of disharmony within the family. And then we wouldn't get any work done, don't you see."

"But it's really no big deal," said Cyrus.

"Cyrus, the Captain thinks it is," snapped Abernathy. "He wants the problem between you and Christopher resolved quickly. Today is

Friday. You have the whole weekend to patch things up. The Captain expects you to have everything resolved when you come back Monday morning. Then people won't be upset about it anymore. Do you understand, Cyrus?"

"Well I can't promise next Monday, Mr. Abernathy. Christopher has gone for the day, and he won't be back until a week from Monday."

"I see," said Abernathy. "Has he gone out of town?"

"I'm not sure."

"You're not sure?"

"He took some annual leave."

"Well did you authorize his taking annual leave, Cyrus?"

Cyrus felt the squeeze coming on, so he told a lie to get out of it. "I authorized his leave before we had our disagreement."

"Well then. If Christopher will be away from his office all week, we might not have as big a problem as we first expected. Still, I think the two of you had better get this matter cleared up as soon as possible. I'll check back with you next Friday, and we'll see how much progress you've made by then. Okay, Cyrus?"

"Yeah, okay."

"Good, Cyrus. We'll get back to you next Friday. Have a nice weekend."

"Horse's ass," said Cyrus as he slammed down the phone. This was not turning out to be one of his better days.

Cyrus knew he had to force Christopher to back down, and he had to do it before Christopher came back to the office. He knew he couldn't reason with Christopher, because there was too much at stake. Cyrus could lose his job if this thing got out of hand. As he saw it, it was either him or Christopher, and Cyrus didn't want to be the one who got fired. So he decided to try to force Christopher out of the company with threats, coercion, or whatever else it took.

Cyrus saw Christopher's decision to take a week off as a real advantage. If Christopher wasn't in the office, he wouldn't be able to dig up any more information. That would give Cyrus time to build a stronger power base within the company, and it would also allow time for Abernathy to cool off.

"Yes," thought Cyrus, "the longer Christopher stays away, the better my position is going to get."

Cyrus leaned back in his chair, put his feet on his desk, and tried to think of what he could do during the upcoming week to harass Christopher. He let his mind wander as he gazed around his office. He looked at his wife's picture on his desk, and for a second he thought about having sex with her. Then he thought about her relatives who he disliked immensely.

"Bunch of slobs," he said to himself. "Especially her sister Thelma. God, what a cow."

Then, as he thought about his sister-in-law and her family, an idea came to him.

"Bruno," he said aloud. "I'll get my stupid nephew Bruno to help me."

Cyrus thought his nephew Bruno was a classic goon. He was six feet two inches tall and weighed 230 pounds. He'd been an all-city football player in high school but wasn't academically qualified to go on to college. So he went to work as a tavern bouncer. He also played touch football in the parkboard league where he'd been suspended a couple of times for dirty play and unsportsmanlike conduct. Besides being a bouncer, he was employed parttime as a security guard for a firm that worked rock concerts at the Met Center. Bruno was assigned to break up fights that got started. He succeeded in his job by beating up the participants and tossing them out the gate. He almost got fired when he broke the jaw of a seventeen year old girl who claimed she was being assaulted by two members of a motorcycle gang.

"What a perfect choice," thought Cyrus. "I'll get Bruno to bounce on Christopher a couple of times. That'll get him off my back. It might even get him out of the company."

Cyrus picked up his phone and called his sister-in-law. After some irrelevant small talk, Cyrus told her he wanted to get in touch with Bruno.

"He's right here," said Thelma. "What do you want him for?"

"Just let me talk to him, Thelma. Please?"

Thelma put down the phone and went to get her son.

When Bruno picked up the phone, Cyrus asked him if he'd like to go to work for him.

"What did you have in mind, Uncle Cy? You know I don't do no hard work," said Bruno with a hearty laugh.

"It's the kind of work you're good at, Bruno. I need someone to help me convince as associate of mine that he should leave our company. There may be some physical labor involved, if you know what I mean."

"Hey, it sounds good, Uncle Cy. When do I start?"

"I need you right away," said Cyrus. "And Bruno, I'd like you to keep this just between you and me."

"How about hiring my friend Chet too?" asked Bruno.

"Two of you? Yes, that might work out all right. Why don't we all get together first thing tomorrow morning and talk about it?"

"Sure," said Bruno. "Where do you want to meet?"

"Why don't you and your friend join me for breakfast about nine o'clock at the Rainbow Cafe over on Lake Street. I'll fill you in on the details then. And remember, Bruno, this is just between you and me. You don't even have to tell your mother. Okay?"

"Yeah, sure," said Bruno. "She wants to talk to you now. I'll see you in the morning."

"Cyrus," demanded Thelma when she got on the phone, "what are you going to do with my boy?"

"He's going to work for me," said Cyrus.

"Are you going to pay him?"

"Of course I'm going to pay him. It'll probably be the best pay he's ever received for the amount of work he has to do."

"From you? Ha! That'll be the day," said Thelma. "But you'd better pay him, and pay him good, or you'll never hear the end of it."

Cyrus thanked Thelma for her advice, said goodbye, and hung up. Then he leaned back in his chair again and thought about his plans for Dick Christopher. He'd never hired anyone to do something like this before, but he thought it was an exciting idea. He imagined all kinds of things. He could see Bruno beating up on Christopher, and he could see Christopher with busted ribs and missing teeth. If Bruno did his job right, Cyrus expected Christopher to quit his job and give up without a fight.

Cyrus' mood improved considerably as he thought about all the things he was going to do to Christopher. He put his feet back on his desk, lit a cigar, and started planning for an exciting week.

It took Dick thirty minutes to drive from his office to his condo-minium in the southwest suburb of Bloomington. He drove into the underground garage and backed into his designated parking stall. His fifteen-foot aluminum canoe was suspended from the ceiling above the stall by a rope and pulley system that Dick had devised. Dick lowered the canoe to the cartop carrier and secured it with hook straps. Then he went upstairs to get the rest of his camping equipment.

The caretaker was starting to paint the backstairs when Dick went up to his apartment, so he decided to get his packing done right away. Otherwise he'd have to go down the front stairs, across the parking lot, and through the garage service door to get to his station wagon.

Dick was always ready to go canoeing, so it didn't take him long to get everything together. His duffle pack already contained a tent, a sleeping bag, clothes, cooking utensils, and other necessities. He wrote out his menu for the week and then filled his food pack with dehydrated provisions he kept in his storeroom cabinet. He planned to pick up some perishable items when he reached Grand Marais at the head of the Gunflint Trail. He also hoped to catch enough fish to supplement the dry food he was taking. Finally, he stowed his binoculars, camera, and sundry items in his day pack. Then he picked up his duffle pack, food pack, and fishing tackle and took them downstairs to his station wagon. When he was all loaded up, he went back upstairs and called Ellen Bishop.

Ellen was a thirty-two year old widow who worked as a stock bro-ker for Dain Bosworth. She and Dick met two years after her husband was killed in an industrial accident. In the three years they'd been going together, they shared many of the same sorrows, because they'd both lost their mates in tragic accidents. But they also shared many of the same pleasures.

They both liked to go camping and canoeing. They also liked to go to athletic events, especially those that involved the Vikings and North Stars. And whenever they had a chance, they watched the Minnesota Gophers play football, basketball, or hockey.

Dick grew up in Minnesota and lettered in five sports in high school. A couple of knee injuries kept him out of college athletics, except for intramurals. Now he played golf and racquetball and spent a lot of time canoeing and hiking. Ellen's interests in athletics came after she met Dick, and now she was as avid a sports fan as Dick was. The two of them also liked to go to concerts and plays, but their first love was for the out-of-doors.

Ellen felt vulnerable after her husband was killed, and she deeply resented the way many men and some older women patronized her. As a result, she got pretty aggressive in searching for a job and relating to other people. At the same time, she retained the charm and poise she'd already developed. The combination had worked well for her. She'd become a stronger person as well as a successful stockbroker.

Dick's wife died twelve years ago in an automobile accident, and it took him a long time to get over the shock of her death. When he met Ellen, his whole life seemed to change for the better. Now the two of them were very much in love. They talked a lot about marriage, but at the same time, they were afraid of losing their independence.

When Ellen answered her phone, Dick invited her to dinner.

"That's not very much notice, Richard."

"I just took it for granted that you'd be coming anyway," said Dick, trying to needle her.

"Don't take anything for granted with me, mister."

"Just teasing, love. I'd really like to see you."

"Why?" asked Ellen, sounding hurt.

"Because I love you, I want to see you, and I want to tell you about the battle I had with Cyrus Bransky today."

"What happened?" asked Ellen.

"It's a long story," said Dick. "I'll tell you about it over a glass of wine."

"Well, I suppose I can come, but I'll have to cancel all the other arrangements I've made for this evening."

"I appreciate the sacrifice," said Dick. "I'll have dinner ready at seven. Why don't you come over before that so we can talk."

Ellen agreed to join Dick for dinner, but only after she'd told him how difficult it was for her to do so. Dick went along with her charade, remembering that they had agreed earlier in the week to get together anyway.

After he hung up, Dick dialed again and called Nelson's lodge on Clearwater Lake outside of Grand Marais. He was pleased to find out that they had one room left in the main lodge for Saturday night. He confirmed his reservation and told the girl on the phone that he'd be there by late afternoon.

After his phone calls, Dick finished the correspondence he brought home with him, paid some bills, and cleaned up his condominium. At six o'clock he started getting dinner ready.

Ellen arrived at six-thirty with two bottles of chablis. She buzzed Dick's apartment and waited for him to let her in through the lobby door. He was waiting for her when she came down the hallway. They gave each other a big hug and a kiss and then Dick took the bag she was carrying.

"What's this?" he asked.

"Chablis. Sebastiani."

"Good. I was going to get some, but I forgot."

"I know," said Ellen as she walked past him toward the kitchen, "You always do. What's for dinner?"

"Chicken Kiev," said Dick. "I got the recipe from the girls at the office."

Ellen laughed and moved into the living room. Dick opened one bottle of wine and put the other one in the refrigerator. He poured each of them a glassful and joined Ellen on the couch.

"Tell me about Bransky," said Ellen as she took her glass of wine from Dick.

Dick told her about his involvement in the integrated-memory system project. He also told her about the article in the company newsletter in which Bransky was credited with developing the system. Then he told her about the confrontation he'd had with Bransky and of the information he got from Matt Weed.

"So what are you going to do now?" asked Ellen.

"The first thing I'm going to do is get the hell out of here. I've decided to go up on the Gunflint Trail for a week and do some canoeing."

"What on earth are you going to do that for?"

"I need to get away so I can think this thing through. Right now there's just too much to sort out. I've got to find a way to come up with the right decision, and being around Bransky won't help. We'd probably end up killing each other before the week was out."

"But if you leave, you'll just make things worse," said Ellen. "Everything you need to make a decision is right here, not up north. You should stay here and settle this thing now. If you run away from Bransky, you'll be under more pressure than ever. And while you're gone, he'll get the upper hand."

"But I don't even know if I want to stay with the company," said Dick. "I don't want to get involved in a big fight with Bransky if I'm going to quit. And besides, I have no assurance that the Captain is going to support me. So even if I win the fight, he might kick my butt out of there."

"Then quit."

"It's not that simple. I've got to break down all the alternatives so I can choose the right one. I need to find the right answer."

"Well you're not going to find it paddling your canoe all over the north woods," said Ellen. "You're just trying to avoid a fight with Bransky. You should be digging in, not running away. Fight it out and take what comes. You can stay, quit, or get fired. But at least you'll know where you stand. *Then* you can go out in the woods and hide. You're looking for an escape, and there isn't any."

"You don't know what I'm going through," said Dick. "It's easy for you to sit back and give advice, but I have to wade through all that crap. And I know it's going to be tough to do. I need to stand back where I can get a real clear look at what I'm facing. I'm too close to it now to be able to see anything."

"I think you're going about it all wrong," said Ellen as she got up to get another glass of wine.

Dick didn't like to argue with Ellen, but then it was difficult for him to be involved in an unpleasant confrontation of any kind. He'd rather compromise and negotiate, and he didn't think Ellen could understand that. He admired Ellen's strength and tenacity, and he sometimes wished he was more like her. But now he was really uncomfortable, because she had pointed out a weakness that he was trying to deny. In spite of his apparent combativeness, he didn't want to get

involved in an all-out fight with Cyrus Bransky.
Dick was disappointed that the evening had started off the way it had. He got up to join Ellen in the kitchen when the doorbell rang. It was Ted Canfield, Dick's next door neighbor.

"Hey Richard, what are you doing," asked Ted. "I saw your wagon with a canoe on it. Are you going on a woodsie?"

"Come on in, Ted," said Dick as he stepped back from the door. "I'm going up on the Gunflint Trail for a few days. I want to do some fishing and canoeing before the summer is over."

"He's running away, Ted," said Ellen as she came out of the kitchen.

"Hi, doll," said Ted. "Are you still running around with this old honkey?"

"Come on, you two," pleaded Dick. "Lay off, will you?"

Ted Canfield was thirty-six years old, a bachelor, and a Minneapolis attorney. He had been an outstanding college football player, but unlike many black athletes, he passed up a promising professional football career and decided instead to go to law school. He and Dick moved into the condominium complex on the same weekend, and they'd been good friends ever since. They often shared each other's quarters when one of them was out of town. That's why Ted was there now.

"I'd better be nice," said Ted, "because I need a favor."

"You're not going to get any favors by calling me an old honkey," said Dick.

"I take it all back, and I am truly sorry if I offended you," said Ted with feigned concern.

"What do you need, you has-been?"

"If you're going to be gone for the weekend, I'd like to use your place. I'm painting both bedrooms and my main bath, and I could sure sleep a lot better if I didn't have to inhale all those paint fumes. I'd like to store some things over here too, like pictures and stuff."

"No problem," said Dick. "I'll be leaving around nine o'clock tomorrow morning, and I'll be gone all week. So bring over anything you've got. Just don't bring over any of those ugly girls you've been dating."

Ellen joined the conversation, and the three of them continued with their good-natured jibes. Then Dick told Ted about his battle with

Bransky, and Ellen accused Dick again of running away. Ted listened as the two went back and forth, and then he called a truce.

"There's no way I'm going to stay here and get shot in the crossfire," he said. "I'm going back to my apartment where it's safe."

After Ted left, Dick and Ellen finished their dinner without discussing the Bransky ordeal again. Their conversation centered instead on Dick's canoe trip. After they finished eating, Dick got out his trail maps, and the two of them worked out a canoe trip for him to take.

The wine and dinner made both of them feel relaxed. Even though it was August and the air conditioner was on, they decided to build a fire in the fireplace. The warm glow of the fire gave them a feeling of euphoria, and soon they were making love. What had started out as a miserable day for Dick was turning into an evening of love and romance.

At eleven thirty, Ellen decided to go home. Dick pleaded with her to stay, but she declined.

"Look, love," she said, "I'd really like to stay, but bright and early tomorrow morning you're going to be crashing around here, getting ready to go up north. And I want to sleep late. So I'm going home, and I'm going to sleep alone."

"I'd behave myself," said Dick.

"I wouldn't want you to if I was here," said Ellen. "Now go to bed. I'll see you when you get back."

Ellen started for the door, but then she stopped and turned back to Dick.

"Promise me you'll be careful," she said.

"Hey, don't look so worried."

"I just don't want you to go away, especially now. I've got an uneasy feeling that something is going to happen to you."

"Don't worry, Ellen. Nothing is going to happen. It's going to be just like every other canoe trip; peaceful, quiet, and enjoyable. Come on, give me a big hug."

The two of them embraced, and Ellen hung on tight. Then she pulled back, gave Dick a kiss, and went out the door.

Dick watched her as she walked through the lobby. Then he went back into the living room and closed the door behind him. He couldn't imagine why Ellen was so worried. Like he told her, it was just a canoe trip. But after he got into bed and turned out the light, he felt the same sense of apprehension he'd experienced earlier in the day. He was still trying to figure it out when he fell asleep.

⚜SATURDAY

Dick woke up early, ate a big breakfast, and got ready to leave for the Gunflint Trail. He carried the last of his food, some sundry items, and his day pack to the basement garage and put them in his station wagon. Then he went back upstairs to tell Ted Canfield he was leaving.

Ted was just fixing breakfast when Dick knocked on his door. He opened it and offered Dick a cup of coffee.

"No thanks, Ted. I just wanted to leave my key with you. Feel free to use my place all week if you'd like. I should be getting back here either Friday night or Saturday afternoon."

"Where will you be in case this place burns down?" asked Ted.

"I'll be staying at Nelson's Lodge on Clearwater Lake tonight. That's up on the Gunflint, right outside of Grand Marais. Tomorrow morning I'll go into the Boundary Waters Canoe Area. If anything comes up, call Sue Nelson, the owner of the lodge. Her phone number is on the itinerary I left on my kitchen counter, but I hope you won't have to use it."

"Okay, buddy," said Ted. "Have a good trip. I'll try not to bust up your place while you're gone."

They shook hands and Dick left for his canoe trip. He still had an uneasy feeling about going, but he thought he'd lose it as soon as he got to the lake country.

Dick didn't know it, but as he headed north, some other people were getting together to make sure his feelings of apprehension would get a lot worse.

At nine o'clock, Cyrus Bransky drove into the parking lot at the Rainbow Cafe. He was met by his nephew Bruno Kruger and Bruno's friend Chet Barta. Chet was not as big as Bruno, but he shared many of the same characteristics. He stood nearly six-feet tall, and weighed about 190 pounds. He and Bruno played on the same parkboard football team. They also worked as security guards for the same company. Unlike Bruno, Chet was continuing his education in an automechanics program at a local vocational/technical school. Chet was tough, and he appeared to be a little smarter than Bruno.

Cyrus made a mistake when he told them they could order whatever they wanted for breakfast and he'd pay for it. Cyrus was not a big eater, and he had no idea how much men that size could eat. And like two kids on vacation, Bruno and Chet went wild. They both ordered steak and eggs with side orders of pancakes and hashbrowns. On top of that, they each had three large glasses of orange juice and several cups of coffee.

Cyrus was amazed at the amount of food they ate, but he was appalled at their atrocious table manners.

When the two of them finally finished eating, Bruno let out an enormous belch that could be heard by everyone in the restaurant. He and Chet thought it was the funniest thing they had heard all day, so they sat there, punching each other and laughing. Cyrus held his head in embarrassement, because everyone was looking at them. Finally, Bruno stopped laughing and turned to his uncle.

"What's up, Uncle Cy?"

"I want the two of you to do me a favor," said Cyrus. "I have a man working for me who needs to be encouraged to leave. I thought the two of you might be able to provide him with proper persuasion."

"You don't mean to beat him up, do you, Uncle Cy?" asked Bruno as he tried to act surprised. He turned and hit Chet on the arm, and the two of them started laughing again.

Cyrus was having second thoughts about the two idiots who were cavorting across from him. He was convinced he'd made a mistake when Bruno let out another horrendous belch.

"All right, you two," said Cyrus. "Knock it off."

"Okay, Uncle Cy. Now, just what do you want us good old boys to do for you?"

"I want you to lean on a man named Dick Christopher. You've got to convince him that he has a much better future with another company. I'm not asking you to do anything violent, but on the other hand, I'm not against your using a little physical persuasion either."

"Can we beat him up, Uncle Cy?" asked Bruno as he laughed and hit Chet again.

"Mr. Bransky, what did this guy do?" asked Chet.

"You don't have to be concerned with that," said Cyrus. "He's just a very disruptive force in our company, and I want him out."

"So why don't you fire him?" asked Chet.

"Because it's not that simple," said Cyrus. "He's a troublemaker, and he'd start raising all kinds of hell if we tried to fire him. We want him out of the company, but we don't want any trouble from him when he goes. That's why I want the two of you to encourage him to leave."

"But can we beat him up?" asked Bruno who seemed to be laughing at everything he said.

"Bruno, you can do whatever is necessary to convince him to leave. But at the same time, I want you to use your head. I don't want you to do something dumb that's going to reflect back on me or the company. I want you to put the fear of God into Christopher, but I don't want you to tell him that I was the one who had you do it."

"But won't he be able to figure that out?" asked Chet.

"He might," said Cyrus, "but I don't want you telling him."

"Okay, Uncle Cy," said Bruno, "we'll do it. Won't we Chet?" Bruno looked at Chet for confirmation of his decision.

"What's in it for us?" asked Chet.

"I'm prepared to make it worth your while," said Cyrus. "I'll pay each of you a hundred dollars."

"Oh come on, Uncle Cy," said Bruno. "You can do better than that for crying out loud. That ain't even worth our time. Is it Chet?"

Chet got up to leave.

"Okay," said Cyrus, "Two hundred. But that's all."

"Make it three hundred apiece and we'll do it. Won't we Chet?"

"Plus expenses," said Chet as he sat down.

"What do you mean, expenses?" sputtered Cyrus.

"Expenses," said Chet. "If we bust something, I sure as hell don't want to get stuck with the cost of fixing it."

"Bust something?" asked Cyrus.

"Yeah, like my hand, Mr. Bransky. I want the three hundred clear. And I want to be covered if I bust something or come up with any other legitimate costs of doing business."

"All right," said Cyrus. "I'll pay it. But you have to take care of it tonight."

"I don't see nothing wrong with that," said Bruno. "It sure as hell shouldn't take all night to bounce a guy around a little. Should it Chet?"

"When do we get paid?" asked Chet.

"I'll give you a hundred now and the rest tomorrow morning. We'll meet back here at the same time."

"At nine o'clock?" wailed Bruno. "That's a hell of a time to have to get up, especially on Sunday."

"Force yourself," said Cyrus. "I'll have the rest of the money for you then."

"Plus expenses," added Chet.

"Yeah, plus expenses," said Cyrus. "Now, I've got to go. Here's the first hundred, and here's Christopher's address. He lives over in Bloomington."

"What does he look like?" asked Bruno.

"He's about six feet tall and weighs about 175. He's got sandy hair with a little bit of gray around the sides. Nothing special. Oh, and he's white, in case you're wondering."

"He'll be black and blue tomorrow," said Bruno.

"Now for God's sake," said Cyrus, "don't screw this up. I'll see both of you back here at nine tomorrow morning."

Cyrus left the restaurant and drove home. He wasn't completely satisfied with Bruno or Chet, but he couldn't think of any other alternatives. He wanted to put pressure on Dick Christopher right away, and this seemed to be the best approach he could think of.

Back in the restaurant, Bruno and Chet talked about the arrangement they'd just made. They both had several ideas on how it should be done, but instead of sitting there and arguing, they got up and left for

Bruno's apartment. They knew they had to get some things together if they were going to finish their job that night.

Cyrus, Bruno, and Chet didn't know that their quarry had already left town. And Dick, who was the object of their pursuit, didn't even know the chase had begun. So from all outward appearances, Cyrus' plan to harass Dick seemed doomed from the start. But Cyrus was a determined man. When he set out to do something, he usually stayed with it, especially if his sense of survival was threatened in any way. So, on Saturday morning, Cyrus' seemingly hopeless plan was put into motion.

While Cyrus was meeting with Bruno and Chet, Dick was heading north out of Minneapolis on Interstate 35. The weather was perfect and the traffic was lighter than he'd expected for a Saturday morning.

Dick felt relaxed during the three-hour trip to Duluth. Every once in a while he'd start thinking about his problems with Bransky, but after a minute or two, he'd change his thoughts to Ellen or to his canoe trip. He knew he'd have to start soon to come up with some solutions, but at the moment, he preferred to think about things that made him feel good.

It was almost noon when he got to Duluth. He left I-35, dropped down to Michigan Street, and bypassed most of the commercial and tourist traffic. He swung back up on Fifth Avenue and caught U.S. 61 heading northeast. From there he continued toward Grand Marais, 115 miles up the north shore of Lake Superior.

The first time Dick came to the Gunflint Trail and the Boundary Waters Canoe Area was when he was fifteen years old. He and a bunch of other kids from his hometown had gone to a YMCA camp on West Bearskin Lake. The camp was still there, looking much like it did when he was there as a camper, twenty-seven years ago.

The BWCA was a real paradise as far as Dick was concerned. And even though it usually took six hours to get there, he felt the drive was well worth it.

The air along Lake Superior was clear and cool. The only clouds

Dick could see were some distant thunderheads to the southeast over northern Wisconsin.

As Dick passed Gooseberry Falls, he thought again about his evening with Ellen. She'd struck a nerve with her assessment of his situation, and in a way, he resented her for it. He didn't think his canoe trip was an attempt to escape from Bransky. He just thought it would help him get ready for the unpleasant confrontation he knew he'd have when he got back. He thought his reason for going was a good one. But when he had tried to justify it to Ellen, she had accused him of rationalizing.

Dick knew he was only about twenty minutes from Grand Marais when he passed the ski area at Lutsen. He started thinking about all the things he needed to do before he went up the Gunflint Trail. He had to get gas, and he had to pick up some groceries. He also wanted to stop and see Lester Malone who'd been a high school classmate of his.

For all the years Dick had been coming to Grand Marais, he never knew that Lester lived there. He learned about it when the two of them met at the twentieth reunion of their high school class. They agreed then to try to get together whenever Dick came up. But as it was, they hadn't seen each other since the reunion. They'd never been real close in high school, but because the school was small and they both liked athletics, they played on most of the teams together. Now, about the only thing they had in common was their love of the outdoors. Dick thought it was time for him to fulfill his part of the agreement. And besides, he was hoping Lester would be able to tell him where the walleyes were biting.

Lester was head custodian for the Cook County school in Grand Marais. During the summer months he also worked as a fishing guide. Five years ago, his wife was asphyxiated by a leaky gas stove in an ice-fishing house. She suffered central nervous system damage that affected her both mentally and physically and left her partially disabled. After it happened, Lester had to work extra hard to pay their medical bills and raise their four children. Dick knew that Lester had been through some pretty tough times.

At two-thirty, Dick came down the hill from the west and entered Grand Marais. The little town of 1300 people looked as inviting as ever. The harbor to Dick's right was filled with commercial fishing boats and pleasure craft. Sea gulls swarmed along the rocky shore. The Coast

Guard lighthouse stood white and gleaming at the head of the breakwater. In many ways, Grand Marais reminded Dick of a New England coastal village. As usual, the streets were alive with hikers, campers, and fishermen.

When Dick saw the stone archway over the start of the Gunflint Trail, he felt as though he were back with an old friend. The Gunflint Trail was really a two-lane asphalt road that left Main Street in Grand Marais and extended north and west for fifty-seven miles through the Superior National Forest to Saganaga Lake on the Canadian border. There were over thirty resorts along the Trail, and some of them were right next to the Boundary Waters Canoe Area.

Congress established the BWCA as a wilderness preserve by setting aside 1,080,500 acres of land and lakes on both sides of the Gunflint Trail. The BWCA extended for over 113 miles from the Pidgeon River on the east, to the Voyageurs National Park on the west.

Dick had mixed feelings about the strict regulations that were used to protect the BWCA. He knew motors could be used on some of the lakes, but only if they were ten horsepower or less. The number of lakes involved was very small and growing smaller, but since Dick didn't have a motorboat, he wasn't really affected by the rule.

He was happy to see the ban against taking bottles or cans into the BWCA. Like most careful campers, he routinely brought out everything he took into the wilderness. So he thought the regulation was a good way of maintaining the beauty of the area. It also helped to eliminate carelessly discarded debris.

Dick was not a hunter, so the restriction on firearms didn't mean much to him. He knew that poachers still worked the area, but they generally used hunting bows and arrows to avoid detection. A rifle shot in the wilderness could usually be heard for several miles.

The use of travel permits really appealed to Dick. The regulation was put into effect to prevent overcrowding of campsites and portages. The number of canoe parties starting out at each of the seventy-five entry points was regulated on a daily basis. Even in the height of the season, Dick could go for days and not see another person.

In spite of all the regulations, the BWCA was well used. Even the camping areas that bordered the BWCA seemed to benefit from the regulations. Almost everyone who came to that part of Minnesota extended their concern for nature to the entire area, not just the BWCA.

Dick wanted to stop and see Lester first, so he drove up the Gunflint Trail to the county hospital and turned east. He found Lester's house two blocks past the school. It was an attractive rambler that stood out from the others in the neighborhood because of the care it received. The yard was well cared for and flowers were everywhere. A late model Chevrolet pickup truck was in the driveway. Dick parked behind the pickup, went to the back door, and knocked.

A large dog came barking to the door. Lester Malone was close behind.

"Dick Christopher! What are you doing here?" Lester was obviously glad to see Dick. "Come on in."

Dick entered the spacious kitchen and shook hands with Lester. "It's good to see you, Les."

"Here, sit down. Let me get you a beer." Lester got two bottles of Moosehead from the refrigerator and brought them to the kitchen table. "I haven't seen you since our twentieth reunion. How long has that been?"

"Four years," said Dick. "Our twenty-fifth is coming up next year."

"I sure don't want to miss that one. Not after the good time I had at our twentieth. Almost every member of the football team was there. And four of us who were starters on the basketball team made it. We should've got a game going."

"I doubt if we'd been able to go very long," said Dick. "Some of those guys looked to be in pretty bad shape. But you still look like you did when you were playing."

"Well you don't look so bad yourself," said Lester. "We could've at least shot a couple of games of twenty-one."

"What do you weigh now?" asked Dick.

"I'm still about 185. I got heavy right after high school when I went into the army. Then after I got discharged, I got a job in Minneapolis and lost it all. I've stayed about the same ever since."

"Didn't you meet your wife in Minneapolis?" asked Dick.

Lester looked out the window as if he was trying to see something far off in the distance.

"Millie and me were married in Minneapolis. That was twenty-one years ago this spring. She sure was pretty then."

"How's she doing now?" asked Dick.

"She's about the same. When she got asphyxiated she suffered some brain damage. She can't remember much from day to day, and she's pretty crippled up. She's just hanging on I guess."

"I'm sorry Les. Is she here?"

"No, not now," said Lester. "My oldest daughter took her for a ride in the van. They'll be gone 'til supper time."

"Are all your kids here?"

"Just Ruth, our oldest girl. Our son Bob is working in a taconite plant over near Hibbing. The other two girls are working and going to school down in the Twin Cities. Ruth stayed home to take care of Millie and never left. We couldn't have done it without her help. Things have been kind of tough on all of us."

"Are you still doing guide work?" asked Dick.

"Some," said Lester, "but not as much as I did when we really needed the money for Millie's medical bills. Now I only go out fishing with some guys from Chicago who come up about three or four times a summer. They pay real good, so I don't have to do as much of it. And I'm doing more work at the school now too, so I don't have the time I did before. But enough about me. What are you doing up here?"

"I'm going to take a little canoe trip," said Dick.

"Where are you planning on going?"

"I think I'll put in on Clearwater Lake and go east from there," said Dick. "I'll go down Caribou, Pine, and McFarland and then come back through East and West Pike."

Lester look surprised. "That doesn't sound very good to me," he said. "I think you'd do a lot better going north out of West Bearskin up to Duncan, Rose, and Gunflint. You'll find good fishing up that way, especially on Duncan and Rose. But you sure as hell aren't going to get many fish going east."

"Well fishing isn't the only reason I have for going that route. I like the area."

"I still think you're making a big mistake going that way," said Lester, "The portages aren't well marked, and the campsites aren't much good either. I've been both ways, Dick, and I really think you should go north."

Dick was surprised at Lester's insistence and said so.

"Hey," said Lester, "all I'm trying to do is help you have a good trip. It's no big deal, but I know you'd be a whole lot happier going north out of Bearskin. As a matter of fact, I don't know why you're even thinking about going out of Clearwater in the first place. I'd think you'd want to start from someplace farther up the Trail."

"I want to stay over at Nelson's Lodge tonight. And besides, I like that part of the Trail."

"Well I'd sure change my mind about going east if I was you. Here, come out to the garage and we'll check my maps. I'll show you where the good fishing holes and campsites are."

Lester got two more bottles of Moosehead out of the refrigerator. Then he and Dick went out to the garage and into an adjoining workshop where the inside wall was covered with a large detailed map of the entire BWCA. Lester asked Dick to show him the route he'd selected. Then Lester pointed out his choice for a better route. The relative merits of both were discussed in detail.

By the time Dick finished his beer, he'd agreed to take the northern route that Lester had suggested. He also agreed to see Lester again at the end of the week before he went back to Minneapolis. Then the two of them said goodbye and Dick went to get gas and groceries.

Dick was glad he stopped to see Lester, but he was puzzled over Lester's insistence about taking a different route. Dick had been on most of the lakes they talked about, and he couldn't see much difference in going north instead of east. It was almost as though Lester had wanted Dick to stay away from the eastern route.

Dick stopped at the Standard station on Main Street and filled up with gas. Then he went to Peterson's market on the highway and got the rest of his perishables. When he was all ready, he headed up the Gunflint Trail for Nelson's lodge on Clearwater Lake.

The Gunflint Trail wound through pine forests, next to shimmering lakes, and over creeks and rivers on its fifty-seven-mile journey north and west from Grand Marais. One place along the Trail in particular was Dick's favorite. About nine miles out from town the road passed through a grove of Norway pine trees that were all over seventy feet tall. To Dick, the trees stood as sentinels to the wilderness beyond. Once he was past them, he felt as though he had entered a completely different world.

After driving for twenty-eight miles on the Trail, Dick turned east on a gravel road. He went three more miles up and down hills, around several sharp curves, and past three other lakes, until he came to the public landing on West Bearskin Lake. Eight cars and three pickup campers were parked there, attesting to the popularity of this starting-off point. The YMCA camp where he had gone as a boy was located on the north shore about two miles down the lake. Except for the late-model cars, the area looked just as it did when he first saw it as a boy.

Dick continued another two miles to Nelson's Lodge, which was located at the west end of Clearwater. This was almost like a second home for Dick. He'd been coming to Nelson's off and on for the past fifteen years. It was clean, comfortable, and well-maintained. And it was considered to be one of the best lodges along the Trail.

The main lodge was built of logs in 1925 and measured sixty by forty feet. Two apartments and four sleeping rooms were on the second floor, and the office, kitchen, dining room, and lounge occupied the fwith floor. A wide, open porch extended across the front and along the east side, which faced the lake. Six other log cabins were scattered around the eighty-acre site. There was also a bunkhouse for the help and a lal maintenance and laundry building.

Even though the cabins were always full, the Nelsons did most of their business outfitting canoeists. They supplied just about everythis a including food, sleeping bags, tents, and canoes. And they served groups of all sizes as well as individuals.

Dick parked his station wagon in the lot next to the main lodge. Then he went up on the porch and into the spacious lobby. Sue Nelson was behind the desk.

"Hello, Dick," she said as he walked through the door. "How was your trip up from the Cities?"

"The trip was great," said Dick. "I had a clear blue sky, cool breezes, and beautiful scenery, just like always. How've you been?"

"Just great. We're full every night, and it's been a real good year for outfitting. You're lucky, you got the last room we had left."

"How about a BWCA permit. I'd like to get one for the West Bear-skin landing."

"Whoops, can't do that. West Bearskin is full until Monday. You'll have to start somewhere else."

"Damn," said Dick. "An old classmate of mine convinced me that Bearskin was the only way to go. What's left?"

"Why not go out of Clearwater? I think it's every bit as good as Bearskin. What's over there anyway?"

"Well actually Clearwater was my first choice. I had originally planned on going over to Caribou, Pine, and McFarland. Then I was going to come back through East and West Pike. But my old classmate said the fishing and campsites were much better going north out of Bearskin."

"I don't mean to argue with your friend," said Sue, "but you'll find everything you're looking for right here. Our people say the fishing is good, and we haven't heard any complaints about the campsites."

"Well that sounds good enough for me," said Dick. "Give me a permit for Clearwater then."

Dick told Sue about the general route he planned to take as she wrote out the permit. When she was finished, she handed it to him along with his room key.

"Here's your permit, and here's your key. You're in room number four at the end of the hall. Oh, and by the way, we're going to charcoal some steaks on the grill tonight. Would you like to join the other guests for dinner?"

"Count me in," said Dick. "I'm so hungry I could eat two."

"Not these you can't," said Sue. "They're a real bellyfull. And besides, we're also having fresh blueberry pie. The kids picked the berries this morning."

Dick thanked Sue. Then he took his day pack and went up to his room. He still had time for a swim, a sauna, and a short nap before dinner. He was glad to be back in the country he loved.

Dick found several people already seated in the dining room when he came down for dinner. He decided to mingle with the other guests, so he joined Bob and Suzanne Montgomery who were seated at one of the smaller tables. Dick introduced himself and learned that the Montgomerys had been coming to Nelson's Lodge for the past fourteen years.

"When did you first come up to the BWCA?" asked Dick.

"I started coming up here when I was fifteen years old," said Bob. "That's thirty-three years ago. I went to a YMCA camp over on West Bearskin."

"Camp Menogyn?" asked Dick. "I went there too, but I must have been there after you."

"How long did you go to Menogyn?" asked Suzanne.

"I only went two years," said Dick. "After that I came up here with some friends from high school. We kept coming every summer through my senior year in college."

"The first time I came up here," said Suzanne, "was when our kids started going to Menogyn. Bob and I have been coming here to Nelson's ever since."

"I assume you both like it here," said Dick.

"I love it," said Suzanne. "We have three boys and a girl, and it's been a great place to raise our family. We started bringing them up here when the oldest was in junior high school. We live in Duluth, so it's not far for us to come."

"Not much has changed in all those years," said Dick. "And I doubt if there will be many changes in the future. It just seems to stay pretty much the same, and I think that's great."

"The people on the trails aren't the same," said Bob.

"What do you mean?" asked Dick.

"We've seen some pretty ugly things up here over the years. Lots of young high school and college kids coming up here to get stoned."

"I would imagine that some of that has been going on for quite a while," said Dick.

"Not like it is now," said Bob. "Sure, we used to bring a six-pack along once in a while when I was a kid. But kids today are bringing in drugs and hard liquor, and some of them are getting killed because of it."

"Two years ago," said Suzanne, "we ran into a real tragedy up here. Four boys who were camped over on Alder Lake were mixing drugs and alcohol. One fell in the lake and drowned. Another one tried to save him, but he fell on the rocks and split his head open real bad. The other two almost died from the combination of alcohol, drugs, and exposure. Two of the boys were in the same school as our kids."

"There have been other instances like that," said Bob. "The year before that happened, a couple of college kids fell into Winchell Lake and drowned while they were high on drugs. I know a lot more kids who've been messed up pretty bad."

"I can't imagine that this area has turned into a hotbed of drug traffic," said Dick.

"I suppose it's not as bad as it is in some of the big cities," said Bob, "but it looks bad up here where it's never happened before."

"Where do you suppose the kids are getting their drugs?" asked Dick.

"I think most of it comes from Chicago," said Suzanne, "although a lot of it is brought in on the foreign ships that come into the Duluth harbor."

"I think a lot of it is coming down from Canada," said Bob. "There are a helluva lot of lakes along the Canadian border, and damn few people are out there patrolling them. Almost every little town between Duluth and Thunder Bay has some kind of drug problem. Again, it's not as big as what you'd find in the cities, but it's there. We've seen it."

Dick had been coming to the BWCA almost as long as the Montgomerys, but he'd never seen any instance of drug or alcohol abuse. The BWCA ban on bottles and cans kept most of the alcohol out of the area. But even in the campgrounds that were outside the wilderness area, he'd never seen problems like those the Montgomery's described. He thought they were oversensitive to the problem because of their kids.

Then he remembered that Lester Malone had gone through some problems with his son. The boy had apparently been arrested several times for buying booze when he wasn't old enough. He'd even been kicked out of school a couple of times. Dick supposed that the boy had also been involved with drugs at sometime or another. So maybe there was a problem in the area that he wasn't aware of. But even if there was, he couldn't consider it as being of major importance. At any rate, he wasn't going to dwell on it.

Dick and the Montgomerys spent the rest of their meal talking about the weather and their favorite lakes and fishing spots. They were good people and Dick enjoyed their company. The T-bone steaks were as big as Sue had promised. Dick ate all of his along with a baked potato, tossed salad, French onion soup, corn on the cob, and several pieces of homemade bread. When the fresh blueberry pie came, he thought he'd better pass it up. But then he knew he wouldn't get a similar treat again for a long time, so he ate a big piece with vanilla ice cream on top. He could hardly move when he finished. The Montgomerys had enough sense to take most of their steak in a doggie bag.

As the last few dishes were being cleared, Sue Nelson came out of the kitchen and sat at their table.

"Did you get enough to eat?" she asked.

"Fantastic as always," said Bob, "but far too much for me to eat."

"I feel like I ate a ton," moaned Dick. "Sue, that has to be the greatest meal I've ever eaten in my entire life. I don't think I'll ever move again."

"You'll wear that off in a hurry," laughed Sue. "It'll only take a couple of days of canoeing and hiking before you'll be starving again."

"A hike sounds like a good idea," said Suzanne. "Come on, Bob, let's hike down to the West Bearskin landing before it gets dark. We could both use the exercise."

After the Montgomerys excused themselves and left, Sue asked Dick if he'd decided where he was going to be camping and fishing.

"I think so," said Dick, "but I'd like to hear your suggestions. Why don't I go get my maps and meet you in front of the fire. Then you can help me pick out the choice spots."

Dick went up to his room, opened his day pack, and got out his canoe maps. The maps were made of waterproof parchment and were designed specifically for canoeists and fishermen. They showed canoe routes, portages, rapids, campsites, and other important details. Dick took them with him and went back to the lounge.

Sue was waiting for him on a couch in front of the fire. He spread out his maps and then described the routes he'd selected.

"I'd like to get in some good, hard paddling the first two days," said Dick. "Then I'd like to stop somewhere and fish for a couple of days. I'm just taking it as it comes, so if I get tired of fishing, I'll move again. I should be back here either Friday or Saturday, depending on the weather and the luck I have fishing."

"Where are you going from Clearwater?" asked Sue.

"From Clearwater I'll portage into Caribou. Then I'll go on to Little Caribou, Pine, McFarland, Little John, and John. I'll try to shoot the rapids between McFarland and Little John and between Little John and John. Then I'll go on to East Pike and camp there Sunday night. I'm hoping that on Monday night I'll be able to camp on the island in West Pike. I might stay on the island Tuesday and Wednesday if the fish are biting."

"That sounds good," said Sue. "Not many people know that there's a campsite on the island, so you shouldn't have any trouble getting it. And I know the bass are biting between the island and the south shore, so you should get some good fishing in too. Where will you go from there?"

"The rest of the week is really up for grabs," said Dick as he scanned his maps. "I've always been interested in this little seventy-acre lake called Gogebic that feeds into West Pike. The Minnesota Fish and Game people stocked it with splake a few years ago, and I'd like to go up there and try to catch some."

"I've been to Gogebic," said Sue. "The trail is steep, narrow, and difficult to find. But it's well worth the trouble if you can get in there. It just might be the kind of place you're looking for."

"If I went to Gogebic," said Dick, "I'd stay there Thursday and come back through Clearwater on Friday. Otherwise, I might go over to Mountain Lake and spend a day there. My goal now is to go down McFarland and then try for the island in West Pike. What I do after that will depend on how the fish are biting."

Dick and Sue sat in front of the fire and talked for several minutes about his trip, the weather, fishing, and canoeing and camping in general. Then Sue had to excuse herself to take care of some lodge business.

Dick sat and gazed at the fire until it almost put him to sleep. Then he thought he'd better get up before he went to sleep in the lounge. He decided to go for a walk to try to wear off some of the food he'd eaten. It was nearly dark when Dick went outside. He walked to the gravel road in front of the lodge, turned east, and continued for three quarters of a mile until he got to the public landing. He only saw three cars there, so he assumed the canoe routes out of Clearwater weren't being heavily used. He was glad of that. And as he thought about it, he was puzzled again at Lester's insistence that he go on another route.

Dick stood at the water's edge and looked out on the glassy-smooth surface of the lake. An almost-full moon was rising around the point behind the trees to his left. He could see a party of two canoes coming in from a half mile out on the lake and wondered where they'd been.

As darkness closed in around him, he turned and walked back to the lodge. The long trip, the fresh air, and the big dinner had all combined to make him very tired. After a warm shower, he climbed into bed and thought about the days ahead. For reasons he couldn't explain, he felt that this trip was going to be the most eventful he would ever take. Then he turned out his light and went to sleep.

◄━━━

While Dick was enjoying himself in the north woods, Bruno and Chet were driving into the parking lot of his condominium in Bloomington. The caretaker was out cleaning up the grounds when Bruno approached him.

"Are you the caretaker?" asked Bruno.

"I sure am."

"I'm from Security Systems Incorporated," said Bruno as he flashed his badge. "We got a report that your security alarm system is acting up. Would you let us in so we can check it out?"

"Sure," said the caretaker. "Do you want me to come with you?"

"No," said Bruno. "We won't need you, because these things usually only take a few minutes to fix. Just show us where the stairs are, and we'll get right to it."

As the caretaker opened the door for Bruno and pointed out the stairway, Chet looked at the directory and found the number of Dick's apartment. Then they both thanked the caretaker, walked to the stairway, and closed the door.

"What's his number?" asked Bruno.

"Two-ten," said Chet. "That's probably on the second floor."

"No kidding," said Bruno. "How'd you figure that out? Come on, you meathead, let's go."

They went up to the second floor, opened the stairway door, and walked down the hall. When they reached Dick's apartment, the door was open, so they walked right in.

"Hey! Is Dick Christopher here?" asked Bruno as he walked through the doorway.

Ted Canfield was just coming out of the bedroom when he met them.

"Who are you guys?" asked Ted.

"Where's Christopher?" asked Bruno.

Chet moved into the kitchen and started looking around.

"Dick's not here," said Ted. "How'd you guys get in here?"

"We're here on business," said Chet. He saw the note Dick had written for Ted and started reading it.

Ted could sense that something was wrong. "Why don't you guys get out of here right now?"

"Hey calm down, buddy," said Bruno. "We're just looking for Christopher."

"Who the hell are you?" asked Ted again.

"We're business associates," said Bruno, "and we want to know where Christopher is." He started moving toward the bedrooms.

Ted put his arm out and stopped Bruno. He didn't like the looks of either one of these gorillas, and he sure wasn't about to tell them where Dick had gone.

"Tell us where Christopher is," said Bruno as he moved menacingly toward Ted.

"He's out of town and won't be back for a week. I don't know where he went. Now get the hell out of here." Ted put his hand against the wall to keep Bruno from moving any further.

Bruno moved forward and jabbed his finger against Ted's chest. "Then how come you're here? I think you know where he is, and I think you're going to tell us or else get yourself a busted head."

Ted brushed Bruno's arm back and pushed him toward the door.

Chet came out of the kitchen, hit Ted along the side of his head with his fist, and sent him crashing against the wall. Then Bruno hit Ted in the stomach, causing him to fall back against the big brass lamp that was sitting on the hall table. Ted tried to steady himself against the table, but only managed to pull it down with him when he fell.

"Get up and tell us where Christopher is," yelled Bruno as he stood over Ted.

Just then, Dick's other neighbor, Ethel Rappaport, poked her head in the door, saw what was happening, said, "Oh my goodness," and hurried to her apartment.

The distraction caught Chet and Bruno off guard long enough for Ted to pick up the lamp and slam it against Bruno's back. That caused Bruno to fall against Chet who was standing in the doorway, looking to see where Mrs. Rappaport went.

Ted swung the lamp and hit Bruno again. As Bruno tried to keep his balance, he grabbed Chet, and the two of them fell on top of each other in the doorway. Ted tried to slam the door shut, but he slammed it against Bruno's foot instead. On Ted's second try, Bruno pulled his foot back and the door slammed shut.

Ted was still woozy from being hit as he stumbled back against the overturned hall table, fell against the wall, and knocked a glass-framed print crashing to the floor. He leaned against the wall, tried to catch his breath, and listened to Bruno and Chet pound on the door.

When another door opened down the hall, Bruno and Chet decided they'd better get out of there. They turned and ran to the rear of the building where they found a stairway door with a "Do Not Use" sign on it. They ignored the sign and started down the stairs.

They had only taken a few steps when they discovered the stairs had been freshly painted. To keep from sliding, they grabbed the handrail and found that it too was covered with fresh paint. When they got to the first landing, they tried the door, but it was locked, so they continued on to the basement.

They opened the basement door and found themselves in the underground garage. As they ran to the outside door, they left a trail of maroon footprints behind them.

When they got outside, they sprinted across the parking lot and jumped into Bruno's van. Bruno started it up, sped out into the street, and cursed the paint that covered his hands, feet, and clothes.

"We blew it," said Chet.

"I'd like to go back there and beat the hell out of that turkey," said Bruno. "He almost broke my goddamn foot. Jeeze that hurts."

"Do you think Christopher was there?" asked Chet.

"I doubt it. If he had been in the back somewhere, he'd have come out when we started knocking that black dude around."

"I saw a note on the counter in the kitchen," said Chet. It said something about somebody going up north on a canoe trip."

"What else did it say?"

"Something about the Gunflint Trail. It also gave the name of a lodge and a phone number. It was Nelson's Lodge, but I don't remember the phone number."

"That must be where Christopher went," said Bruno. "We'd better tell Uncle Cyrus that his friend took off on us. But first we've got to get rid of this goddamn paint. Jeeze I'd like to kill that son of a bitch. This is the worst mess I ever got into."

"Oh I don't know," said Chet. "I kind of like the color."

Bruno almost ran off the road when he swung at Chet and missed.

🦆 SUNDAY

After Dick's alarm went off at six o'clock, he lay in bed for a few minutes and listened to the cry of a loon that was coming from somewhere out on the lake. It was an unmistakable call, and he considered it his official welcome to the north woods.

Reluctantly, Dick got up and went down the hall for the last warm shower he'd have in a week. After he shaved, he went back to his room and got dressed. He could hear someone stirring in the kitchen below and knew that the lodge would soon be full of activity.

He walked quietly down the wooden steps so he wouldn't waken any of the other guests. Then he stepped out on the porch, checked the temperature, and walked over to his station wagon. He unhooked the tie-down straps and slid his canoe across the cartop carrier. Then with one quick motion, he lifted the canoe above his head and dropped it down on his shoulders. The portage yoke felt comfortable to him as he carried the canoe down to the dock. When he got to the water's edge, he flipped the canoe up, over his head, and down to his knees. Then he quietly eased it into the water, next to the dock. After securing his canoe, he went back to his station wagon for the rest of his gear.

Years of experience had led Dick to select lightweight equipment that did what it was supposed to do. He didn't take anything he didn't need, and everything he took had its place in the canoe. The duffle pack, containing Dick's tent, sleeping bag, clothes, cooking equipment, and food pack, was stowed under the bow seat. Dick secured it with the tie-down straps he'd used to hold the canoe to the cartop carrier. The spare canoe paddle and Dick's fishing tackle were strapped to the stern thwart. He kept his day pack under the stern seat where he could get to

43

it while he was paddling.

When he had everything ready in his canoe, he went back to the lodge for breakfast. Two couples were sitting at one of the smaller tables, so he got another table by himself. No one else was in the dining room.

In spite of the big dinner he'd eaten the night before, Dick felt hungry. He knew he wouldn't be eating like this again for several days, so he ate everything that was brought to him, including eggs, sausage, blueberry pancakes, fresh wild raspberries, orange juice, and lots of coffee.

As he was finishing his third cup of coffee, he heard the phone ring in the office. He was surprised and a little apprehensive when Sue said the call was for him. It was Ted Canfield.

"Good morning, Dick. I'm glad I caught you before you took off into the woods."

"What's up?" asked Dick.

"I didn't want to bother you, but I thought you should know what's been going on down here. A couple of goons came by your place last night while I was moving my stuff in. They said they were looking for you, but they were obviously looking for trouble. We tussled a bit and some things were broken."

"Are you all right?"

"Yeah, I'm okay," said Ted. "The brass lamp in the hall and your print both got busted, but I'm more concerned about you. One of the goons read the note you left in the kitchen. I don't know how much he saw or even remembered, but I think they know you're up there."

"Do you know who they were?"

"I never saw them before. They're big dudes and real mean, but not too smart. I think they have something to do with your run-in with Bransky."

"Why do you say that?"

"They said they were business associates of yours, and it happened the day after you and Bransky went at it."

"I can't believe Bransky would do something as dumb as to send someone out to beat me up," said Dick. "But I suppose if he's scared enough, he'll do just about anything. Maybe I'd better come back down there and get this straightened out."

"No, you don't have to do that," said Ted. "You'll just get a busted head. Stay up there and relax. I'll try to find out what's going on. And even if those clowns know you're up there, I doubt if they could find you. But to play if safe, you'd better keep looking over your shoulder so you don't get ambushed."

"What do these guys look like?" asked Dick.

"Like I said, they're big. One is about six-two and maybe 230. The other is about six-foot and maybe 190. You'll know who they are when you see them together."

"Okay, Ted, I'll stay up here. But you'd better be careful. I don't want anything to happen to you on my account. If you have any other problems, call Sue Nelson here at the lodge. She'll give me the message when I come back in at the end of the week."

Ted told Dick he'd try to find out more about the two men who were looking for him. Then he wished Dick a safe trip and hung up.

Dick told Sue about his call. "I think those two might be coming up here to look for me."

"I'll watch for them," said Sue. "Maybe we can distract them or get them to go somewhere else. I'll tell the help to keep their eyes open and to take down any messages if your friend Ted calls back. But you'd better be careful."

"Don't worry, Sue. Those guys aren't going to find me. And even if they do, I think I can handle myself all right."

Dick said goodbye to Sue and went down to the dock. It was eight-thirty, the sky was clear, and a slight breeze was coming out of the west. Dick made one last check to see that everything was secure. Then he got into his canoe, pushed off from the dock, and started to paddle toward the Caribou portage.

Dick thought right away about the phone call he got from Ted. Someone was apparently out to get him, but it was hard to believe that Bransky was responsible. If Bransky did hire those two goons, then it was because he was worried about the information Dick had. Or else he was just spoiling for a fight. Dick didn't think Bransky would go so far as to send those two all the way up to the BWCA. But on the other hand, he knew Bransky was capable of doing just about anything.

Cyrus had to wait a half hour at the Rainbow Cafe before Bruno and Chet showed up. Neither of them had much to say as they joined Cyrus at a table in the back.

"Well," asked Cyrus, "how'd it go?"

Bruno and Chet looked at each other, but neither one said anything.

"I asked you guys a question."

"We didn't see Christopher," said Bruno. Then he told Cyrus what had happened the night before. Cyrus was furious.

"How could you two be so goddamn dumb?"

"What do you want us to do now, Mr. Bransky?" asked Chet.

Cyrus wasn't sure. He wondered if Christopher already knew that Bruno and Chet had roughed up his neighbor.

"Did you find out where Christopher was?" he asked.

"I saw a note in the kitchen," said Chet. "He apparently went canoeing somewhere on the Gunflint Trail. The note said he was starting out from Nelson's Lodge, wherever that is."

Cyrus knew Christopher did a lot of canoeing in the wilderness area of northern Minnesota. If that's where he went, then Cyrus was in an even better position. Christopher wouldn't be around to dig up any more information about the Atchison contract, and Cyrus could spend the whole week mending his fences.

But Cyrus didn't want to leave it at that. If Bruno and Chet could catch up with Christopher in the north woods, they could get away with anything. The thought of terrorizing Christopher really excited Cyrus, so he decided to continue with his plan.

"Okay, you guys," said Cyrus, "you're going to go on a little trip. I want you to go after Christopher, run him down, and let him know we don't want him back."

"What are you talking about?" asked Bruno. "Do you mean you want us to chase all over the north woods looking for some guy that you're pissed off at?"

"That's right," said Cyrus. "The man you roughed up last night is probably a friend of Christopher's. You can be damn sure he's already tried to let Christopher know that the two of you are after him. Christopher is probably shaking in his boots right now, so I want you two to stay after him."

"That's crazy," said Bruno.

"Don't tell me it's crazy, you pinhead. I want to make sure that when Christopher comes back to town he's already made up his mind to leave the company. You two are going to convince him. You're already in this, and you're going to stay in it until it's done."

"What if we don't?" asked Bruno.

"If you try to get out of this now," said Cyrus, "I'll make it miserable for both of you. You need me, and I need you. And besides, I'll make it worth your while so you won't want to get out."

"Yeah? Like how?"asked Chet.

"I'll pay each of you $100 a day *plus expenses*. You get a nice vacation in the north woods, and at the same time do what you do best—bust some guy's head in."

"One-fifty or we don't do it," said Bruno.

"Forget it," said Cyrus.

"You need us, Uncle Cy. You just said so yourself. If we get in trouble for what we did last night, we'll just say you made us do it."

"One-fifty sounds right for what you're asking us to do," said Chet. "That's a helluva big area, and we're going to have to work our butts off trying to find this guy."

"Okay, one-fifty a day and expenses," said Cyrus. "But you'd better not screw up this time or I'll have your heads."

"So what do you want us to do?" asked Bruno.

"First of all," said Cyrus, "you have to find out where Christopher is. I doubt if he's still at that lodge, but call anyway and make sure. If he's not, then he's probably out in the woods somewhere. If you contact the Forest Service, they should be able to tell you how to find him. As soon as you know where he is, rent a boat or a canoe and go after him. There have to be places up there where you can get everything you need."

"That's going to take some cash, Uncle Cy."

Cyrus got out his wallet and took out some bills. "Here's $500," he said. "That'll pay for getting up there and renting the equipment. I'll pay you the rest when you get back."

"When do we start?" asked Chet.

"Today," said Cyrus.

"Tomorrow," said Bruno, "first thing in the morning. I've got some things I have to do before we go. Besides, I've got a buddy who goes up there a lot. We can see him today, and he can tell us where to go and what to get."

"Okay," said Cyrus, "that's it then. But remember, I don't want you two screwing this up. Understand? Give me a call when you get back. And the sooner you get back the better. I don't want this going on much longer."

Cyrus got up and left the restaurant.

"This is crazy," said Chet after Cyrus had gone.

"I know it is," said Bruno, "but what the hell. It's an easy way to pick up some change, and we get to go someplace where we've never been before."

"But I don't know nothing about canoeing," said Chet.

"Neither do I", said Bruno, "but don't worry about it. My friend will show us everthing we need to know. Hell, little kids are doing this all the time. If they can do it, we sure as hell ought to be able to."

"But what if we don't find Christopher?" asked Chet.

"We still get a nice vacation, compliments of my Uncle Cyrus."

"And what if we do find him?"

"I don't know," said Bruno. "Bust his ribs, sink his boat. We'll think of something."

"I think your uncle has been watching too many gangster movies," said Chet. "This whole thing is crazy. Christopher will know right away that your uncle is behind it. How does he think he'll get away with it?"

"Don't worry about Uncle Cyrus," said Bruno. "I know for a fact that he's done a lot worse things than this. And even when people knew he screwed 'em, they never pressed charges or anything. He just gets away with it whenever he does it."

"That's hard to believe," said Chet.

"Oh I don't know," said Bruno. "I did something like this when I was bouncing at a bar over in northeast Minneapolis. It was owned by three guys, and two of them wanted to cut the third man out. They tried to pay him off, but he wouldn't go. He knew about the skimming that was going on, and he wanted to sue the other two. So they asked me to encourage him to leave."

"What did you do?" asked Chet.

"I met the guy in the parking lot one night after we closed up and told him he was to cut out. He starts giving me a bunch of crap, so I hit him in the ribs a few times. I knew I broke some, because I could hear 'em crack. Then I kicked him a couple of times and slammed him against his car. I just looked him in the eye and told him to get the hell out of town. The other two guys gave me some money to give to him, so I shoved it in his pocket and stuck him in his car. He took off and they never saw him again."

"And we're supposed to do that to Christopher?"

"Do whatever you want. Just so he decides to leave the company and not bother my Uncle Cyrus anymore. Now come on, we've got to get some things done if we're going canoeing."

Bruno and Chet got up and left the Rainbow Cafe. The chase was on, but the odds weighed heavily in Dick Christopher's favor. Neither Bruno nor Chet had ever been in a canoe before, their camping experience was nil, and they had to find Dick in the middle of a million-acre wilderness they had never been to before. Understandably, Dick Christopher was not too concerned. At least not yet.

Dick paddled smoothly over the ripples in Clearwater Lake. The muscles in his shoulders, arms, and back responded easily to his efforts even though he'd not been on a lake for two months. Ahead of him, the early morning sunlight spread across the water like millions of sparkling diamonds. The clear, cool water felt invigorating when it splashed on his hands. Like so many times before, he felt excited about starting off on another canoe trip.

After he'd gone a mile, he rounded a point of land and entered a sheltered cove. He glided noiselessly across the smooth surface and looked for the Caribou portage on the far shore. He recognized it right away by the noticable depression in the skyline. Foilage had been cut back from the shore, revealing what looked like the entrance to a cave. The only other means of recognition was a half-submerged log that extended out from the water's edge and served as a landing dock. The Forest Service sign that identified the portage had probably been stolen long ago by a souvenir hunter.

Using his paddle as a pole, Dick eased up against the log and beached his canoe. The silence of the cove was broken by the telltale sound of his aluminum canoe scraping against the gravel lake bottom. Keeping one hand on the canoe for balance, Dick carefully stepped on top of the wet log, walked to shore, and pulled his canoe up behind him. He moved his duffle pack to the stern thwart and fastened it securely. Then he put on his day pack and tied it snug to his waist. After he stowed his fishing gear and two paddles under the bow seat, he was ready to move out.

Dick's use of lightweight equipment allowed him to carry everything on one trip. It almost doubled the weight of his canoe, but it saved a lot of time, especially on long portages.

He stood on the left side of the canoe and lifted it to his knees. Then, with his right hand on the left end of the portage yoke, and his left hand on the right end, he quickly lifted the canoe up, over his head, and onto his shoulders. He moved his hands out to the gunwales ahead of him, bounced the canoe a couple of times until he felt the balance was right, and started down the Caribou portage.

In his younger days, Dick could carry his canoe the entire length of a portage without stopping, but now he stopped wherever the Forest Service provided a rest. On most portages, that meant at least two or three stops. The rests were nothing more than horizontal supports that were attached to a tree about eight feet above the ground. When Dick set the front of the canoe on the support and the rear of the canoe on the ground, he could step out from under the canoe and rest his shoulder muscles. After a few minutes, he'd lift the canoe away from the support and continue on the portage.

It took Dick twenty-five minutes to reach Caribou Lake. When he got to the end of the portage, he set his canoe down, eased it into the water, and looked out onto the lake. Since he couldn't see anyone else, he thought he was probably the only person on the three-mile lake. Being alone like that made him feel good and gave him the opportunity to do a lot of thinking.

After he arranged his gear so the canoe would be balanced, he pushed off from shore and started to paddle again.

Suddenly, two bald eagles left their shoreline perch and flew no more than thirty feet above his head. He quickly got his binoculars out of his day pack and followed the birds in flight. One kept climbing until it disappeared over the back ridge of the palisade on Clearwater Lake. The other one perched on a dead shoreline tree about a mile down the lake. Dick kept watching the majestic bird as he paddled toward it. When he was about a quarter of a mile away, the eagle swooped down and pulled a fish out of the water. It was quite a sight, and one that Dick knew many people wouldn't see in a lifetime.

Dick made good time paddling down Caribou Lake, and the short portage between Caribou and Little Caribou only took him ten minutes. As he paddled down Little Caribou, he saw a large whitetail doe foraging at a campsite on the north shore. The deer looked at him as he went by, but when she saw he was harmless, she went back to feeding.

When Dick got to the end of the portage between Little Caribou and Pine Lake, he stowed his canoe in the woods about twenty feet from the water. Then he hiked for half a mile up a narrow path that ran along the south side of a shallow tributary. The path ended at the bottom of Johnson Falls. Here, in this beautiful setting, water flowed out of Rocky Lake and dropped 180 feet over rocks, boulders, and three vertical spillways on its way to Pine Lake. The two lower spillways were both forty feet high, and between them was a deep pool from which Dick gathered several leeches to use as live bait.

Dick stayed at the falls for several minutes and watched the rushing water. It was a beautiful spot. And yet, Dick knew that fewer than a dozen people came here each year. Reluctantly, he returned to his canoe and started down Pine Lake.

The sun was almost straight above him now, and he was starting to get warm. He took off his windbreaker and stowed it in his day pack. Then he rolled up the sleeves of his Pendleton shirt and applied a liberal coat of suntan lotion. He knew he could be burned as much from the reflective glare off the lake as from the direct rays of the sun, and he didn't want to spoil his trip by getting sunburned.

About three quarters of the way down Pine Lake, Dick stopped on a little peninsula that jutted out from the north shore. He pulled his canoe onto the sandy beach and got out to stretch his legs.

Dick had undergone surgery on his right knee after he'd aggravated and old football injury, and it tended to get stiff and sore after he'd been canoeing for an hour or so. Now, during this short break in his canoe trip, he walked along the shore and tried to relieve the arthritic pain that was starting to bother him.

Dick was all alone on a beautiful lake that was six and a half miles long and over a mile across. From where he stood, he could see the west end, four miles to his right, and the east end, two and a half miles to his left. The only sound he heard was that of water lapping gently against the shore. Occasionally a breeze would come up, causing a curtain of ripples on the lake and a gentle whisper in the pine trees behind him. Dick was almost overwhelmed by the peace and solitude of that spot.

He thought back to what the Montgomerys had said at dinner the night before, and he couldn't imagine why anyone would come to such a beautiful place to get high on drugs or alcohol. He could get high just by absorbing the beauty and tranquillity that surrounded him.

He walked, stretched, and rested for about fifteen minutes. Then he got back into his canoe and continued down the lake. He hated to leave that spot, but he knew another one just as nice would be waiting for him further on.

Dick reached the end of Pine Lake after almost two hours of paddling. Instead of portaging over to McFarland, he paddled through the short, shallow rapids that connected the two lakes. On McFarland he saw some fishermen who'd come up the Arrowhead Trail from Hoveland. He also passed the Wilderness Lodge on his two and one-half mile trip to the east end of the lake. Then he shot the rapids between McFarland and Little John and again between Little John and John Lake. They were not challenging rapids, but it was exciting and fun for him to go through them.

When Dick got to the west end of John Lake, he faced the rugged half-mile portage to East Pike. The trail climbed 100 feet between the two lakes, and Dick used every rest stop he could find along the way. He was worn out when he reached the shore of East Pike a half hour later, but he was anxious to get to a campsite. So without waiting, he put his canoe into the water and headed down the lake.

A short time later, he reached a pleasant campsite on the north shore. It was on a narrow point of land that faced the east end of the lake a mile and a half away. By camping there, he could see the sun when it came up in the morning.

Dick unloaded his canoe, put up his tent, and started a fire. When he had everything out of his canoe, he stripped to his shorts and went for a swim. The cold, bracing lake water freshened and invigorated him, but he was afraid his muscles might tighten up, so he got out after only fifteen minutes. He dried himself, got dressed, and exchanged his boots for camp moccasins. He wished he had a sauna. Dick stayed close to the fire and fixed a hearty meal of fresh vegetables and beef stew. Sue Nelson was right, his appetite had returned after a full day of paddling and portaging. He enjoyed the meal, but he hoped his next dinner would include fresh walleye.

When he finished eating, he washed his cooking utensils and stowed them under his overturned canoe. Then he took steps to make sure he wouldn't be bothered by bears. He walked back from shore and tossed a nylon rope over a tree limb about twenty feet above the ground. After he tied one end of the rope to his food pack, he hoisted it up to within five feet of the branch. Then he tied the other end of the rope to an adjacent tree. He knew that as long as his food was inaccessible, the bears would probably leave him alone.

As the sun set in an almost cloudless sky, Dick added more wood to the fire and then poured a capful of brandy from his flask. He sat on a tree stump, watched the fire, and soaked up the atmosphere.

"It's good to be here," he said aloud. "It's so much easier to think things out when I'm in a place like this." He said it almost to convince himself that it was true.

He thought about Ellen, and wished she was there with him so she could understand why he chose to come to the BWCA. He thought about Bransky too, and of the confrontation they had. The likelihood of another heated exchange bothered him very much. He didn't want an all-out fight, but he couldn't think of any other way out. He sure as hell wasn't going to negotiate if Bransky had gone so far as to hire two men to harass him.

Dick still found it hard to believe that Bransky had done such a thing. In some ways, Dick thought it was funny, but he felt bad that Ted Canfield had been caught up in it. He was also upset that some of his furniture got busted.

Dick tried to think of the options he faced and the consequences that awaited him, but he was still having a hard time unraveling all the different elements that were involved. He preferred to sit by the fire, watch the moon come up, and think about Ellen.

By nine o'clock the fire was almost out. It had been a long day for Dick, and he was very tired. He wanted to get an early start in the morning, so he decided to go to bed. After taking a last look at the moon, he put out his fire, and crawled into his tent. It didn't take him long to get undressed and inside his sleeping bag. It took even less time for him to fall asleep.

While Dick was enjoying his day in the north woods, Cyrus Bransky was planning strategy back in Minneapolis. He wanted to build a broad base of support in case Christopher decided to come back to work, and he wanted to make sure that most of that support came from Timothy Abernathy and the Captain.

Cyrus was glad that Christopher had gone for the week, because it gave him more time to plan his moves. But at the same time, he felt uncomfortable about having to rely on his nephew for help. He just hoped Bruno and Chet wouldn't do something dumb that would screw everything up.

Bruno and Chet spent a couple of hours Sunday afternoon getting ready for their trip up north. Part of that time was spent with Bruno's friend who'd been camping before. But Bruno was a poor listener, so he didn't absorb much of what his friend told him. He was also egotistical enough to think he could do whatever was needed in spite of what he heard.

Chet was a better listener, but he was totally out of his element. Much of what he heard meant nothing to him.

Neither Bruno nor Chet had any understanding or appreciation of what lay ahead for them. They both thought Cyrus' idea of running down Christopher was crazy, but they were willing to go through with it because of the money they were getting. Between the two of them, they figured they'd have no trouble at all in finding Christopher and convincing him to leave the company.

The stage was set for an exciting week. Cyrus Bransky was directing a clandestine venture, the likes of which he'd never been exposed to before. Bruno and Chet were about to conduct a search for a man they'd never seen, in an area they'd never been to before, using means that were totally alien to them. And Dick Christopher, who sought peace and quiet in the pristine wilderness, was about to have one of the most harrowing experiences of his life.

MONDAY

Dick was awake at six o'clock just as the sun was coming up over the trees at the east end of the lake. From somewhere off in the distance he could hear the early morning call of his friend the loon.

Dick opened his tent, stuck his head outside, and took a deep breath of cool, crisp air. Then he stripped naked and walked gingerly across the dew-covered rocks to the edge of the lake. Without hesitating, he dove in, swam about thirty feet away from shore, turned around, and got back up on the rocks, all in less than a minute. He lathered his body from head to toe with soap and dove back in again. He bathed quickly, rinsed himself off, and hurried back inside his tent.

In spite of the morning chill, Dick felt great. He felt even better after he put on his Levis and Pendleton shirt. As soon as he got his boots and socks on, he gathered twigs and small branches for kindling, added a couple of logs, and got a fire going.

He laughed to himself when he remembered the first time Ellen had come camping with him. His morning bath had always been a ritual with him, but she wanted no part of it. She told him it was obviously an advanced stage of insanity. The only pleasure she got from it was when she zipped the front flap of the tent shut and wouldn't let Dick back in after he'd been in the water.

Dick took down his food pack and fixed breakfast of bacon and eggs, bisquits, and hot chocolate. The early morning cooking smells made him hungrier than he already was. When he finished eating, he washed his utensils and stowed them in his duffle pack. Then he fixed another cup of hot chocolate and got out his trail map. He pulled up a log next to the fire, sat down, and tried to figure out what he was going

57

to do for the rest of the day.

His muscles were still sore from paddling and portaging the day before, so he decided to do less canoeing and more fishing. If no one was camped on the island on West Pike, he'd stay there until Wednesday morning. That would give him plenty of time for fishing as well as a chance to explore Gogebic Lake. If the island was already occupied, he'd go back to Clearwater and then over to Mountain and Rose Lake.

Dick finished his hot chocolate, washed out his Sierra cup, and put out his fire. Then he packed his sleeping bag and tent and loaded his canoe. At eight-fifteen he pushed off from shore and headed for the west end of the lake. By nine o'clock, he'd reached the half-mile-long portage to West Pike. It took him about twenty minutes to cover the portage and put his canoe in the water. By nine forty-five he was approaching the island on West Pike and was happy to see that no one else was camped there.

The island, which was shaped like a boomerang, was only fifty yards long and thirty yards across at its widest point. The inside curve fanned out into a shallow gravel bed that extended almost to the south shore of the lake. The outer curve of the island faced north and was covered with shale. About three feet from the north shore the lake bottom dropped off quickly to a depth of 100 feet. Even though the island was small, it was covered with a surprising number of trees that provided shelter from the prevailing northwest winds.

Dick paddled around to the south side of the island and eased his canoe ashore. He selected a flat, grassy area close to the water as a place to set up his tent. He knew he wouldn't have to worry about bears on the island, so he stowed his food pack in the tent with the rest of his gear. As long as his tent was up, other campers would know the island was occupied and would continue on their way.

Dick was excited over the thought of having a shore lunch of fresh walleye, so it only took him twenty minutes to get his fishing tackle ready. When he was set to go, he went to the north side of the island and picked up a ten-pound piece of shale to use as an anchor. Then he got in his canoe, pushed off from shore, and began fishing between the island and the south shore of the lake.

Dick put everything out of his mind except thoughts of fishing. He didn't allow himself to think about Bransky or work or anything else. He was enjoying himself too much to be concerned about the problems that waited for him back in Minneapolis. But his pleasure would be short-lived, because things were starting to happen that would soon put an end to his feelings of peace and quiet.

Bruno and Chet left Minneapolis for the Gunflint Trail at nine o'clock in the morning. They drove Bruno's van up Interstate 35 to Duluth where they stopped for gas and something to eat. They got lost twice trying to find their way out of Duluth on U.S. 61. Then they were arrested for speeding right outside the little town of Beaver Bay. They finally made it to Grand Marais around three-thirty in the afternoon. When they saw the Forest Service headquarters building at the west end of Main Street, they pulled into the parking lot, parked the van, and went inside.

They asked the young woman behind the counter how they could find Dick Christopher. They said Dick was camping alone somewhere in the BWCA, but they didn't know where. She told them that whenever anyone went into the BWCA, they had to have a travel permit. If they knew when and where Dick had started, she could probably find his permit.

"I think he started yesterday," said Bruno. "And he was going to Nelson's Lodge on Clearwater Lake, wherever that is."

It only took the young woman a few minutes to find a copy of Dick's permit.

"You're right, sir. He got his permit at Nelson's. He started Sunday morning and is scheduled to be back at Nelson's by Friday night. Here, I'll show you where that is on the map."

She came around the counter and went to a large map of the lake region that covered most of the wall.

"Here's Clearwater Lake," she said, "and here's the public landing at the west end. That's probably where he started."

Bruno said to Chet, "At least we know he isn't at Nelson's Lodge anymore." Then he turned back to the young woman. "Where would he go from there?"

The young woman thought for a moment before she answered.

"You said he was alone, so I don't think he'd go to Caribou or Rove Lake. Those are tough portages for one person because they're so long. He'd have to make two trips; one to carry his canoe, and one to carry his camping equipment. He might have stayed at one of the campsites on Clearwater, or he could've portaged over to Mountain Lake. He might even have gone on to West Pike. That's a very nice lake."

"Goddamn," said Chet. "Look at all those frigging lakes. That's a helluva big area to find anybody in."

"Well if I were you," said the young woman, "I'd start looking on Clearwater. There are eight good campsites there, and he could be at any of them. Then I'd go on to West Pike. You can ask people along the way if they've seen him. Chances are that someone would notice him if he's traveling alone. Then if you don't see him on Clearwater or West Pike, you can go over to Mountain Lake on your way back."

"Goddamn," said Bruno. "What a job."

Bruno and Chet got their own travel permit. Then they thanked the young woman, left the building, and got back into Bruno's van.

"I still think this is crazy," said Chet. "Did you see all of those goddamn lakes? We could be out here all summer and still never find Christopher."

"Not me," said Bruno. "I told Uncle Cy we'd only stay up here a couple of days. I'm going to be back in Minneapolis by Friday night whether we find him or not. Now let's go get some camping equipment."

They drove down Main Street to the Gunflint Outfitters. Bill Olson, who owned the store, had been renting and selling camping equipment for twenty-eight years, and he had seen all kinds of people come up to the Gunflint Trail. But he'd never before seen a pair like Bruno and Chet. It was obvious to Bill that they'd never been camping before, even though they acted like they knew everything. And they couldn't seem to get rid of their money fast enough.

Bill rented them a canoe and a cartop carrier. Then he outfitted them with a two-man tent, sleeping bags, cooking utensils, and plenty of dehydrated food. He tried to sell them some misquito repellent and suntan lotion, but neither one of them would take it. Finally, he gave them a guide book on canoe camping and hoped they'd read it before they started out.

The next stop for Bruno and Chet was Peterson's grocery store. They felt they had to add to the food supply they got from Bill Olson, and since they were on an expense account, they decided they might as well get some T-bone steaks. They also bought a lot of candy, potato chips, peanuts, and assorted junk food.

Their last stop was the municipal liquor store, where they bought two cases of beer and two quarts of bourbon. They were completely unaware of the regulation against taking any bottles or cans into the BWCA. But even if they'd known about it, they probably would have ignored it.

Finally, after they bought everything they could think of, they started up the Gunflint Trail, drinking beer along the way and tossing their empty cans out the window. Chet drove and Bruno directed him, using the map Bill Olson gave them. When they'd gone twenty-eight miles, they found the gravel turnoff to Clearwater Lake and headed east. Bill told them they couldn't camp at the public landing, but they wanted to see for themselves.

They passed Aspen Lake, Wampus Lake, the Flour Lake Campground, and the West Bearskin landing. When they got to Nelson's Lodge, Chet stopped the van.

"What are you stopping here for?" asked Bruno.

"I think we ought to go in and see if Christopher is still here," said Chet.

"The lady told us he left here Sunday morning. So why are we stopping?"

"Because I sure as hell don't want to go paddling all over these goddamn lakes when the guy we're looking for is right here."

"Well you go and check. I'll stay here and finish my beer. Be sure and let me know if you see him."

Chet parked the van next to the lodge and went up on the porch. One of the coeds who worked at Nelson's during the summer was behind the desk when Chet walked in.

"Hello," she said. "Can I help you?"

"I hope so," said Chet. "I'm looking for a friend of mine. His name is Dick Christopher, and I think he's staying here."

The young woman checked the register and then turned back to Chet. "I'm sorry, he's not here anymore. He checked out yesterday morning." Then she remembered what Sue Nelson had told her about the men who were looking for Dick.

"I . . . don't know where he is," she stammered. "I mean . . . I . . . he went out on a canoe trip. But I don't know where he went."

Chet didn't notice that the young woman was very frightened. He thanked her and went back to the van.

"He's not here," he said to Bruno. "The girl inside said he left yesterday morning."

"I told you so," said Bruno as he tossed his empty beer can out the window onto Nelson's yard. "Let's go look at the public landing."

Chet continued to drive down the road to the landing on the north side of Clearwater. When they saw it was only a gravel parking lot and not suitable for camping, they turned around and went back to the Flour Lake campground.

There were thirty-four campsites at the campground, but only ten were occupied. The campers who were already there were camped down by the lake. Bruno and Chet decided to pitch their tent on a campsite that was in the back corner of the campground, right off the outer-perimeter road. They were the only people back there, so they had lots of campsites to choose from.

The wooded campground stretched out in front of them for over 100 yards down to the shore of Flour Lake. Behind them, a dense forest of trees and underbrush came right up to the rear edge of their campsite.

They selected one site for camping, and they parked Bruno's van at another site across the road. Then they got ready to spend their first night ever of camping in the woods. It was to be an adventure they'd remember for a long time.

⸺

While Chet and Bruno were being introduced to the north woods, Dick was having an excellent day of fishing. By late afternoon he'd caught and returned several smallmouth bass. But best of all, he had two beautiful walleyes that he kept for dinner.

He only saw one other party on the lake all day. Two men paddled by from west to east around noon. Since he didn't see them again, he assumed they'd gone on to East Pike. He was surprised and pleased that he hadn't seen more people.

Dick stopped fishing around five o'clock. He paddled back to the island, beached his canoe, and got a fire started. Then he cleaned and filleted his walleyes on the west end of the island and left the entrails for the sea gulls. When he had everything ready for dinner, he stripped and went for a swim. The cool water refreshed him and the swim allowed him to get some exercise after sitting in his canoe all day. After swimming for twenty minutes, he got out of the water and stood by the fire as he toweled himself dry. As soon as he got dressed again, he started cooking.

Like thousands of other fishermen, Dick felt that a fresh walleye dinner, cooked outdoors next to a lake, was one of the best meals a person could ever have. He covered his fillets with a light batter, added a little oil, and panfried them over the fire. He added hashbrowns and bisquits and ended up with a fantastic meal. When he finished eating, he cleaned his cooking utensils, poured a capful of brandy, and stretched out by the fire.

Dick was really enjoying the BWCA. It was moments like these that made him feel at peace with himself and the world around him. As he sat by the fire, he thought about all the earlier trips he'd taken over a twenty-seven year period. They all seemed to have made a deep impression on him, and he couldn't think of a bad trip in the bunch. But it had taken years of canoeing and camping experience to develop the skills that made it all work so well.

Dick knew of other people who hated to go camping. Many of them had only gone once or twice, and they complained about everything. They hated the rain, the mosquitoes, the long portages, and the hard days of paddling. They weren't able to see the good things that were happening to them. They tried to fight the elements, and invariably they lost. But Dick had learned to live with nature. And because he could do that, he always ended up with a good trip, even when he ran into bad weather, lousy fishing, or any other problems. As long as he accommodated himself to the demands of the wilderness, he knew he'd come out all right.

Dick was an experienced camper who knew what he was doing. On the other hand, Bruno and Chet were absolute greenhorns. It wasn't hard to see the difference a little experience and common sense made in the way the three of them were adapting to the wilderness. And needless to say, Bruno and Chet were having some problems.

⌣

As soon as Bruno and Chet got their tent up, they decided to take time out and drink some beer. Neither one of them was really stupid, nor were they physically unable to do what had to be done. But they were total strangers to wilderness camping. And trying to live comfortably outdoors was a lot different than anything else they'd ever done before.

They especially lacked camping etiquette. Instead of tossing their empty beer cans in a trash container, they crumpled them in their fists and threw them at each other. It didn't take long for them to get drunk and disorderly.

"Hey, egg-sucker," yelled Bruno, "are you going to cook dinner, or do I have to?"

"I will," said Chet, "because I'm a helluva lot better cook than you ever thought of being. I'll fix a couple of steaks, some french fries, salad, and lots more to drink. But first we need to build a fire, so why don't you go get some wood?"

"Why don't you screw yourself?"

"Come on, you meathead. If I'm going to cook, you're going to have to do more than sit on your fat butt and drink beer."

"Okay," said Bruno, as he stumbled off in search of wood. "I'll build your goddamn fire."

Chet opened the rear door of the van and got out the steaks, a package of frozen french fries, a head of lettuce, and a bottle of salad dressing. He set the food on the picnic table and went back to the van to get the cooking kit they bought from Bill Olson. The kit contained a one-quart kettle with a lid, two plates, a seven-inch frypan, a pot lifter, and two plastic eight-ounce cups. They had forgotten to get knives, forks, or spoons.

The steaks weighed a pound and a half each. That was too big for the frypan, so Chet decided they should be cooked on a grill. But the only thing they had that even resembled a grill was the Forest Service fire grate. The grate was good for holding pots and pans, but it was not intended to be used as a grill for steaks. It was dirty and greasy, and there was no way to regulate the heat.

Chet made another trip to the van and got his old hunting knife out of his knapsack. It was dull and rusty, but it was the only knife he had.

"I found a woodpile," said Bruno as he came back to the campsite with an armload of wood. "We've got all the wood we need. Where's the matches?"

"I don't have any matches," said Chet. "I don't even have any silverware. Go look in the glove compartment."

Bruno found the matches and came back to light the fire. "Have you got any paper?" he asked.

"Use the grocery bags," said Chet.

Bruno went back to the van and tore up all the grocery bags. He left the door open and came back again to start a fire. He shoved the torn paper under the grate, piled five logs on top, and lit the paper.

"Hey," yelled Chet, "what the hell are you doing? I have to cook there." He kicked the logs off the grate and stomped out the burning paper.

"If you're so goddamn smart," said Bruno, "you start the fire." He got another can of beer and went over and sat on the picnic table and pouted.

Chet gathered several twigs and sticks, placed them on one of the grocery bags, and started a small fire. As soon as it was going good, Bruno came over to make it bigger. He added more wood until the flames were rising about a foot above the grate.

"Okay," said Bruno, "let's eat."

Chet filled the frying pan and kettle with frozen french fries and set them on the grate. In a matter of minutes they were both covered with soot.

"We can only cook one steak at a time," said Chet. "There isn't room enough for two."

"Then do mine first," said Bruno.

Black clouds of sooty smoke billowed upwards as soon as fat from Bruno's steak hit the burning logs. The hot grease also loosened layers of soot and dirt that had built up on the grate over the years. Chet tried to turn the steak over with his hunting knife, but he kept getting a face full of smoke. He finally found a stick he could use, but by then the steak was seared on one side. As soon as he turned the steak over, grease hit the logs again and more smoke and soot filled the air. The frypan and kettle were now entirely black, so Chet took them off the fire grate with his stick and set them on the ground.

"It looks done," said Bruno as he surveyed the charred remains of his steak. "Let's eat."

Chet used his stick to shove the steak onto Bruno's plate.

"I need your knife," said Bruno.

"Well so do I," said Chet.

"So how the hell am I going to eat this?"

"Use your frigging fingers," said Chet. "That's the way you usually eat anyway."

Chet tried to loosen some french fries from the bottom of the pans, but most of them were stuck fast. Those that were loose were still cold. He gave those to Bruno anyway.

"Goddamn, this is terrible," said Bruno. "Haven't you ever cooked steaks before?"

"Hell yes," said Chet. "But I never cooked in a lousy, stinking place like this before. And if you don't like it, you can do the cooking."

The two of them argued continuously while Chet tried to cook a steak for himself. The more they argued, the more they drank. They finished one case of beer and started in on the bourbon. Bruno was upset about not having any ice or soda, so he started drinking boilermakers.

They ate what they could of the cold french fries and charred steaks. Neither one of them remembered the lettuce for salads, so it remained untouched on the picnic table. By ten o'clock, they had consumed a case and a half of beer and a quart of bourbon.

Chet got their sleeping bags out of the van and brought them to the tent. After lots of yelling and swearing at each other, they finally managed to get themselves and their sleeping bags into their two-man tent. Then, with their fire still burning, the campground littered with beer cans, and the rear door of the van wide open, they collapsed fully clothed on top of their sleeping bags and fell asleep.

The bears, who had been watching this scene from the woods, waited until it was quiet. Then they made their move.

Back on the island, Dick put out his fire and got ready for bed. The lake was calm, and the nearly-full moon glistened in the cloudless sky above him. Dick could hear a barred owl calling from the trees on the south shore of the lake. Otherwise there was only the quiet stillness of the north woods.

Dick was torn between savoring the delights of a beautiful evening in the wilderness, and getting a good night's sleep. But when he thought of the energy he'd need in the days ahead, he decided to call it a day and go to bed. With one last look at the world around him, he turned and crawled into his tent. It didn't take him long to get undressed and into his sleeping bag, and within minutes, he was fast asleep.

Dick had come to the north woods to escape from problems that plagued him at work. So far, he'd been successful. But he still had lots of concerns that had to be worked out. And unfortunately for him, the days ahead would leave little time to think about anything other than his own survival.

⟨TUESDAY

Lying between West Pike on the south, and Mountain Lake on the north, was a long, narrow, spring-fed pond. It didn't appear on any canoe maps, because it was small and inaccesible. It was about 300 yards long and thirty to forty yards across. At the most, it was only about four feet deep. Forest animals came to this little pond quite frequently. So did a French Canadian bush pilot named Jean-Paul Larouche.

Jean-Paul had been flying his float plane to the pond once or twice a month and usually came before dawn. On this Tuesday morning he was there again with his friend Pierre Druin. He flew in very low, cut his engine shortly after he touched the water, and glided to the west end of the pond.

Pierre scrambled from the cockpit to a pontoon and then to shore where he anchored the plane to a tree. Jean-Paul carried two large packs from the plane and gave one to Pierre. Then the two men hiked down a narrow path that led to the north shore of West Pike Lake.

Near the water's edge, they removed cedar boughs and a dark green tarpaulin from an aluminum canoe that had been hidden earlier. They loaded their packs into the canoe and set off across the lake.

They reached the south shore of West Pike just as the sun was starting to break above the horizon. Passing a beaver dam, they headed for the mouth of a small stream that cascaded down from the hills above the lake. When Jean-Paul beached the canoe, Pierre jumped out and pulled it ashore.

Pierre was a short, powerfully built man who was very strong. He put his arms through the straps of one pack and swung it easily to his back. Then he grabbed the straps of the second pack and started swinging it between his legs like a pendulum. With one quick motion, he swung it up and over his head where it rested on top of the other pack. Then, with Jean-Paul carrying the canoe, the two men started up the narrow trail that followed the stream.

After an uphill hike of almost a quarter of a mile, they came to Gogebic Lake. They checked to see that no one else was around, and then they put their packs in the canoe, got in, and paddled to a shallow area at the west end of the lake. In the predawn haze, they beached their canoe, pulled it through the marshy grass, and left it on shore. Then they took the two packs and headed down a narrow trail into the woods.

After walking about 250 yards, they came to a small pond. They followed the north shore of the pond to the edge of a clearing. There they hid the two packs under the branches of a fallen spruce tree. Using their knives, they cut fresh boughs and placed them on top of the packs. When the packs were well concealed, they returned to Gogebic and paddled back to the trailhead.

Jean-Paul again took the canoe on his shoulders as he and Pierre went carefully and quietly down the trail to West Pike. They knew this remote area was seldom used for camping, but they still preferred not to be seen or heard if they could help it.

When they reached West Pike, they got into their canoe and paddled across to the north shore. No one else was on the lake, but it looked to them as though someone was camped on the island to their right. As soon as they reached shore, they pulled their canoe into the woods and covered it up again with the dark tarpaulin and cedar boughs. Then they hiked up the trail to their airplane.

Jean-Paul started the engine, taxied slowly to the east end of the pond, turned around, and took off. As he did, he banked sharply to the right over Mountain Lake and the Canadian border. He and Pierre would be back in Thunder Bay in less than thirty minutes. Anyone who saw their airplane would probably think it belonged to the Forest Service.

Dick woke suddenly and thought he heard the sound of an airplane. That surprised him because only Forest Service planes were allowed to fly below 4,000 feet over the BWCA. And they usually didn't make their regular run over the area until midafternoon.

Dick stuck his head outside the tent and noticed that the sun had just come up. He looked all over, but he couldn't see an airplane anywhere. He couldn't hear one either, so he thought he must be dreaming.

The morning air was crisp and clear. A slight breeze rippled across the lake in front of his tent and whistled through the pine trees that covered the island. It looked like it was going to be another glorious day.

Dick stripped naked, got a bar of soap and a towel, and went in for his morning bath. The soreness had gone from his muscles, so he swam a little longer than usual. As soon as he was dressed, he got a fire going and started breakfast.

He had been pleasantly surprised the day before when he discovered wild-raspberry bushes on the island, but he was still trying to figure out how they got there. He picked a potful of the bright red berries and made raspberry pancakes and bisquits. He ate what he could for breakfast and saved the leftovers for a midday snack.

Dick was still hungry for walleye, so he got out his fishing tackle and set out for another try at catching lunch. If his luck turned bad, he'd go up and explore Gogebic.

As Dick got ready to go fishing, he took out his binoculars and scanned the lake. He saw a small whisp of smoke rising from a campsite on the north shore about a mile and a half to the east. He couldn't see anything to the west, so he decided to fish in the west end of the lake where he'd be alone.

⌣

While Dick was getting ready to go fishing, Lisa Murphy and Judy Miller were fixing breakfast at a campsite on Rose Lake, twelve miles northwest of Dick. They had taken a week out of their summer to hike the rugged Border Route Trail that wound through the BWCA. This was the start of their sixth day on the Trail.

Both women were experienced campers who'd been coming to the BWCA for the past nine years. They went on their first canoe trip with their parents when they were thirteen years old. In the early years, they both attended a girl's camp over near Ely at the west end of the BWCA.

Then, during their summer vacations from St. Olaf College, they joined other young women on canoe trips to northern Minnesota and southern Canada. They'd just graduated two months earlier, and this was to be their last trip together before they started their new jobs.

The subject of bears came up while they were fixing breakfast.

"Did you hear that bear last night?" asked Lisa.

"I heard something banging around outside," said Judy. "If it was a bear, I'm surprised you didn't invite it into our tent."

"It was a big bear, and I think it was looking for our food pack."

"How do you know it was a big bear? All we've seen so far are yearlings."

"I just know it was a big one," said Lisa. "You wait, we'll see one before this trip is over."

"I don't care if we see one or not," said Judy. "I think we're a lot better off if we leave them alone."

"Well I want a picture of one," said Lisa. "For all the years we've been coming up here, I never got a picture of a bear."

"But you've seen lots of bears, Lisa. Why do you have to have a picture of one?"

"Because I don't have one, and I want one. That's why I brought my flash camera along."

"Maybe you could get a big old sow bear to sit still long enough for you to draw it," said Judy.

"Funny girl. What I really need is a picture of you sitting on a bear's lap."

Judy burst out laughing at Lisa's suggestion, especially when Lisa tried to act it out.

As soon as they finished breakfast, they wasted no time in packing their gear. They had a long day ahead of them and they were anxious to get started. The Border Route Trail they were on ran from the west end of Loon Lake to the public landing on Little John Lake, a distance of thirty-two miles. They hoped to reach the end of the Trail in the two days they had left.

Their hike would take them along the south side of Rose Lake, down the long portage between Rose and Rove Lake, and across the ridge bewteen Watrap and Clearwater. They hoped to cross the portage between Clearwater and West Pike by midafternoon. Then they wanted to find a good campsite somewhere along the ridge above Pine Lake.

Their enthusiasm in getting started was not shared, however, by two neophyte campers at the Flour Lake Campground.

⎯

Bruno and Chet were in a foul mood when they woke up at eight o'clock. They weren't used to sleeping on hard ground, and they weren't prepared at all to sleep in the confined space of a two-man tent. As a result, they hadn't been able to sleep very much. Beside being tired, they were very hungover.

Most of the other campers in the Flour Lake Campground were already fixing breakfast and getting ready for a day of hiking or fishing.

Chet needed to get some fresh air, so he tried to get out of his sleeping bag, turn around, and go out the tent headfirst without bothering Bruno. But in doing so, he stepped on Bruno's face and almost started another fight. Chet had left his boots and socks outside the tent the night before, and when he found them, they were cold and wet with dew. He wanted to take a hot shower, but there wasn't one available.

Chet couldn't believe the looks of the campsite. After they'd gone to bed, the bears had climbed into the van, eaten all their food, and scattered debris everywhere. Even the hot chocolate packets were torn open. He and Bruno had apparently been so drunk when they went to bed, that they hadn't heard any of it.

Chet got some clean clothes, his travel kit, and a towel out of his knapsack and headed for the lake. The water was colder than he'd expected, and it made his head throb even more. He felt better after he washed his hands and face and brushed his teeth, but his head was still ringing from the effects of too much beer and bourbon. He walked back to the campsite and surveyed the mess the bears had left. The smell of fresh coffee and sizzling bacon drifted up from the other campsites and almost drove him nuts.

Chet got matches out of the glove compartment, picked up some of the torn paper that lay on the ground, and built a fire. After he got it going, he added several logs, and soon it was burning outside the fire grate. He was finally warm, but he was almost sick with hunger.

He found the blackened, greasy cooking utensils where the bears had left them. The smell of soot and grease almost made him sick, so without washing the utensils, he hurriedly put them back in the pack. He was so desperate for something to eat that he considered begging from the other campers.

After a lot of effort, punctuated with obsenities, Chet was able to roust Bruno. Together they folded their sleeping bags and tent and stowed them in the van. The campground was a mess when they left it, and Chet's fire was still burning strong.

They drove out of the campground and onto the gravel road that headed back toward the Gunflint Trail. By now they were both having hunger pangs. They not only needed something to eat, but they also needed to replenish their food supply.

They knew there was nothing back toward Grand Marais, so when they got to the blacktop, they turned north and headed further up the Trail. They'd only gone four miles when they came to Halfway House. It was a combination restaurant, grocery store, gas station, bait shop, and laundromat. To them it was an oasis. They ate a big breakfast, bought more food and beer, and drove back to the Clearwater landing.

It took them quite a while to get their canoe down from the cartop carrier, load it up, and put it in the water. Neither one of them had ever paddled a canoe before. And even though they both felt capable of doing so, they weren't very good at all. Bruno started out in front with Chet in back. Both of them tried to steer at the same time, but all they did was work against each other. They blamed each other whenever they started going in circles, and as a result, there was a lot of yelling and swearing going on. Several times, Chet inadvertently splashed cold water on Bruno's back with his paddle. They almost capsized every time Bruno tried to retaliate.

They were both terrified of the middle of the lake, so they stayed close to shore as much as possible. At Bruno's insistence, they headed for the first campsite they saw.

A young couple had just finished breakfast when the two of them paddled up.

"Good morning," said the young man.

"Hello," said Bruno. "Have you seen anybody camping out here by himself?"

"Not in the last couple of days."

"Are you sure?" asked Bruno.

"Well yes," said the young man. "We've been over into Canada for the past five days, so we haven't seen much of anybody."

"Okay," said Bruno as he turned back to Chet. "Let's go." The two of them splashed off to the next campsite.

"They sure don't look very nice," said the young woman. "I wonder who they're looking for."

"I don't know," said her companion, "but they're going to have a heck of a time finding anybody the way they're going."

Bruno and Chet spent the rest of the morning checking out the other campsites on Clearwater. It took them until noon to cover the seven-mile-long lake and reach the West Pike portage. The only reason they found it was because two other canoeists had just come over it and were starting up Clearwater. Bruno yelled at them.

"Hey! Have you guys seen anybody camping by himself on the next lake?"

"On West Pike? Sure," said one of the canoeists. "Somebody's camping by himself on the island about three-fourths of the way down the lake."

Bruno wanted them to stop and tell him more about the camper they'd seen, but they paddled swiftly off.

"If that's him," he said, "we'll get him."

"You know," said Chet, "we really don't even know what he looks like. All we have is your uncle's description to go by. So how are we going to know if it's him when we see him?"

"I'll know," said Bruno. "Just keep paddling."

They paddled to the landing and ran the canoe up on shore. Bruno got out first. Then Chet stood up and started walking toward the front of the canoe. He had only taken two steps when Bruno decided to pull the canoe further up on shore. That caused the canoe to tip. And Chet, who was trying to step over their packs, lost his balance and fell into the lake.

"You dumb son of a bitch," yelled Chet as he stood dripping wet in two feet of water. "What the hell are you doing?"

Bruno was laughing too hard to answer.

Chet charged out of the water and swung his fist at Bruno. As Bruno stepped back to avoid Chet's swing, he tripped on a rock and fell to the ground. Chet pounced on him and the two wrestled in the dirt. Then Bruno, who was still laughing, got to his feet. He liked to fight, and he was ready to continue anything Chet wanted to get started. Chet knew this and decided to back off.

"Goddamn dumb ass," yelled Chet.

"Well watch where you're going," said Bruno. "Now get your butt in gear and let's move this stuff to the next lake. You take the canoe."

Bruno picked up the packs and paddles and left Chet to handle the canoe by himself. Chet pulled the canoe out of the water and tried to lift it to his shoulders. He tried twice, and both times he dropped it to the ground. Then, with no help at all from Bruno, he finally got it up.

Bruno started down the portage at a fairly good pace. Chet came right behind, but he was having a hard time balancing the canoe. First it would tip backwards and the stern would bounce against the ground. Then Chet would try to compensate by tipping it forward, and the bow would dig into the trail ahead of him. He kept this teeter-totter action going for several yards. Then, while he was trying to keep the canoe balanced, he didn't see where he was going and tripped over a tree root. He went crashing to the ground with the canoe on top of him.

Bruno was way ahead of him on the portage, so Chet had to get back up himself. He was already under the canoe, and all he had to do was stand up, but that was easier said than done. It took him two tries before he was back on his feet with the canoe on his shoulders. His right knee was bleeding, and his pants were torn where he'd hit a rock when he fell. As soon as he got the canoe balanced, he limped off down the trail after Bruno. When he finally got to the clearing at the end of the portage, Bruno was there to greet him.

"Where the hell have you been, Chet? We've got to get moving. We can't screw around wasting time all day."

Chet was close to boiling. His shoulders were sore from carrying the canoe over a half mile of rugged terrain. His knee hurt. He was hungry, wet, and still hungover. And he was very pissed off at Bruno. Instead of easing the canoe into the lake, he raised it over his head and threw it. It landed on its side halfway out of the water.

"What's the matter with you?" asked Bruno.

"I hurt, I'm wet, and I'm hungry," said Chet. "And before I do anything else, I want something to eat."

"Okay," said Bruno. "Don't get so upset. If you want to eat, we'll eat. If Christopher is on this lake somewhere, he'll probably still be there a half hour from now."

The two of them looked out across the lake toward the east, but they couldn't see the island that was over two miles away. If they'd been able to see that far, they'd have seen a very contented Dick Christopher. But Dick wouldn't have been so content if he knew that Bruno and Chet were about to pay him a visit.

Dick spent most of the morning fishing from the west end of the lake back to the island. The lake current moved fairly fast from west to east, particularly along both sides of the island. A slight breeze from the west added to the current and kept Dick moving faster than he wanted, so he dropped the anchor he'd made with his nylon rope and the piece of shale. The anchor didn't stop him, it just slowed him down enough to where he could troll very effectively.

At noon he came back to the island for a shore lunch of fresh walleye. As far as he was concerned, there was no greater treat for a fisherman than pan-fried fish, cooked out in the open. After lunch he washed his cooking utensils and set them out to dry in the sun. Then he lay back on the grass alongside his tent and tried to figure out his plans for the future. He thought that as long as he was enjoying the solitude and quiet of the island, he'd stay there one more day before he looked for another campsite.

His solitude was suddenly interrupted by the sound of voices. He looked up and saw a canoe coming toward the island from the west. The canoeists had a breeze at their backs, but they obviously weren't taking advantage of it because they were straying all over the lake. Neither one of them seemed to know how to keep the canoe on a straight course.

Dick took out his binoculars and looked to see who they were. As soon as he focused on them he knew they were the two men Bransky had sent after him. They looked dirty, sunburned, and mean. He thought he could outsmart them, but at the same time he thought he'd better get out of there. When he saw how they were paddling, he knew he could outrun them as long as he had a head start.

He packed his gear as fast as he could and had just finished loading his canoe when Bruno and Chet were about twenty yards out. He went to meet them as they paddled toward him.

Instead of going to the beach on the south side of the island, Bruno and Chet came in on the shale and rocks on the northwest corner. Dick welcomed them to the island and helped them steady their canoe as they came ashore. Bruno was direct and to the point.

"Who are you?" he asked.

"Glen Adams," said Dick.

"Adams, huh? Have you seen anybody else out here? One man camping by himself, like you?"

"As a matter of fact, I have," said Dick. "A man came by here yesterday from Clearwater. He wanted to know how long I was going to be here on the island. I told him I'd already been here three days and was going to leave today. I have to go over to Clearwater so I can catch up with the rest of my group."

"The rest of your group?" asked Chet. "Aren't you alone?"

"No," said Dick. "There are five others in our party. I stayed here an extra day to do some more fishing. The others went over to Mountain Lake.

"Anyway, this man said he'd be back this afternoon. I guess he wanted to camp here by himself. Is he a friend of yours?"

"Yeah," said Bruno, "he's a friend." Then he turned to Chet. "That's probably him."

"Well I was just leaving," said Dick, "so you can wait here for him if you want. It isn't much, but there's firewood and wild raspberries. And the fish are biting over against the south shore."

"Hey, that sounds great," said Chet. "Let's wait for him here."

"Do you know this guy's name?" asked Bruno.

"I'm not sure," said Dick, "but I think he said Christopher, or something like that."

"That's him," said Chet. "Come on, Bruno, let's stay here and wait."

"Okay," said Bruno, "but that son of a bitch better show up."

"Come on," said Dick, "let me help you unload your gear."

When the canoe was empty, Dick went back and made sure it

wasn't pulled up on the rocks. Then he went to his own canoe and shoved off while Bruno and Chet were busy putting up their tent. Dick waved to them as he started up the lake, but they ignored him. He rounded the west end of the island and soon was out of their line of sight. As he came alongside their canoe, he took his fishing rod and dropped a lure in front of the rear seat. Then he paddled out toward the middle of the lake, letting out line as he went.

When Dick was about ten yards from shore, he stopped paddling and started to reel in his line. The lure hooked under the seat and held firm. Dick set the brake on his reel and started paddling again toward the middle of the lake. Bruno and Chet's canoe slipped away from shore with hardly a sound.

When Dick was about a quarter of a mile out in the lake, he turned and looked back toward the island, and there were Bruno and Chet, yelling, swearing, and shaking their fists at him. He couldn't hear what they were saying, but he knew they were mad. And he knew they would be on the island for quite a while.

When Dick reached the middle of the lake, he stopped paddling and reeled in his line until the other canoe was next to his. After he unhooked his lure, he took the piece of slate he'd been using as an anchor and set it in the rear of the other canoe. Then he gave the canoe a shove and watched it glide down the lake. The slate acted as ballast and kept the canoe on a steady course. Dick thought it would beach somewhere along the north shore, about four miles from the island.

Bruno and Chet watched helplessly as their canoe drifted down the lake. Then they watched Dick paddle toward the Clearwater portage.

"That son of a bitch," said Chet. "Why did he go and do something like that?"

"Because he didn't want us to beat the crap out of him," said Bruno.

"But we didn't do nothing to him."

"You idiot, that's Christopher."

"It is?" said Chet. "I thought he said his name was Adams."

"He was lying," said Bruno. "And when I catch up with him I'm going to break him in two."

"What are we going to do now?" asked Chet.

"We'll wait until somebody comes by who can help us get our canoe back. And that had better be damned quick. I want to get back to Clearwater and catch that bastard."

But Dick wasn't going to Clearwater. He headed instead for Gobegic Lake where he was sure nobody would ever find him.

As Dick neared the end of West Pike, he got out his trail map and looked for the trail to Gogebic. He found the small, seventy-acre lake about a quarter of a mile south of his present position. The trail between Gogebic and West Pike ran along the south side of a tributary that connected the two lakes. Gogebic was spring-fed, and according to his geological survey map, it was almost a hundred feet higher than West Pike. There were no designated campsites on Gogebic, but Dick knew people had camped there before.

Dick paddled along the south shore of West Pike until he came to a small inlet. Someone had apparently been there earlier, because he could see where a canoe had been beached. He could also see boot tracks going along the stream that came down from Gogebic.

Dick paddled his canoe ashore and looked for the trail. When he found it, he saw that it was very steep and narrow, and probably too hard to make in one trip. So he stashed his gear in the woods, hoisted his canoe to his shoulders, and started up the hill. He hoped no one else was at the lake ahead of him.

It was a difficult climb even without a canoe. Dick had to back up and cut across the trail several times because of the sharp curves and switchbacks. He also took some bark off the trees when he hit them with his canoe. The trail was obviously not a regular portage, but there was enough torn bark to indicate that someone else had come that way with a canoe before he did.

It took Dick twenty minutes to go from West Pike to Gogebic. He arrived at the north shore and set his canoe down in a small clearing. There were tracks in the area, so he knew someone had been there earlier. But as he looked out over the entire lake, he could see that no one else was there now. He took a few minutes to catch his breath, and then he went back down the trail for the rest of his gear.

The second trip was a lot easier than the first because his vision wasn't blocked by the underside of his canoe and he could see where he was going.

When Dick got back to Gogebic, he loaded his canoe, put it in the water, and pushed off from shore. As he did, he heard the sharp slap of a beaver's tail echo across the water.

He paddled to his left where the sound came from and found that beavers had built a dam across the outlet to West Pike. There were three old beaver lodges near the dam, so he stopped at each one and gathered a supply of beaver wood. He selected several pieces that had been in the sun for a long time. They were the driest and the best for firewood.

Dick found an ideal campsite along the south shore about halfway down the lake. It was in a small, grassy clearing that ran right to the water's edge. There was no beach, just a straight four-foot dropoff to the lake bottom. Beyond that, the gravel bottom fanned out for several yards before it dropped quickly to a depth of fifty feet. It looked like a great spot for swimming and bathing.

Dick beached his canoe, pulled it ashore, and set up camp. After he finished, he noticed a trail behind him that followed the edge of the lake in both directions. He was curious to know where it went, so he took the eastern route toward the beaver dam to check it out. When he got to the end of the lake, he discovered another campsite that looked like it hadn't been used for quite a while. He wandered around, did some exploring, and then headed back. It was getting late in the afternoon, and he knew if he wanted fish for dinner, he'd have to start fishing right away or he'd go without.

⌣

Meanwhile, Lisa and Judy had crossed the Clearwater-West Pike portage at four o'clock and were heading south on the Border Route Trail. The section they were on was a lot harder than they had anticipated, and they were running behind schedule because of it.

South of the portage the Trail climbed 100 feet above Clearwater Lake to the crest of a hill. Beyond that, the Trail leveled out ahead of them as it ran along the ridge between West Pike and Pine Lake. The hill they were on continued to rise gradually to the west for a half mile where it formed the top of the 250-foot palisade on Clearwater Lake. The view from the top of the palisade was spectacular. A person could see all of Clearwater and several other lakes beyond.

When Lisa and Judy got to the top of the hill, Judy asked to stop.

"I don't know about you, Lisa, but I'm really bushed."

"I am too," said Lisa, "but we've got a ways to go before we can find a good campsite for tonight."

"Well I've got to sit here and rest for a minute."

"Okay," said Lisa. "I'll check around and see if there isn't someplace up here where we can camp. You stay here. I'll be right back."

Lisa walked a few yards further, found signs of a deer trail, and moved to her left, away from the palisade and into the woods. The trail widened as it continued through a grove of aspen trees. Then it opened into a small clearing. On the far side of the clearing was a little pond of clear water. Lisa thought it would be a great spot to camp, so she hurried back to tell Judy.

"Come on," she said. "I've found a campsite."

"Up here?" asked Judy.

"Yes, and it looks great. Come on, I'll show you."

The two of them went up to the clearing and checked it out. The distance from north to south was about forty yards, and it was close to fifteen yards from the tree line on the west to the pond on the east. The pond was surrounded on three sides by large pine trees. On the north side of the clearing they found several wild raspberry and blueberry bushes.

"This is bear country," said Judy. "Look at all those berries."

"Great," said Lisa. "We'll eat them all before the bears find them."

Judy was still apprehensive. "This looks like a wildlife cafeteria. Look at all those trails."

"Don't worry, Judy. If a bear comes, I'll take its picture and scream. And nothing alive can stand to hear me scream."

Judy finally agreed to stay, but she made sure their tent was pitched at the south end of the clearing, away from the berry patches. While she was setting up camp, she noticed another trail that led away from the clearing along the south shore of the pond. If any bears came to the berry patches across the clearing, she planned to use that trail as her escape route.

There was no Forest Service grate in the clearing, so Lisa and Judy cooked their evening meal on their single-burner propane stoves. After dinner they spent an hour picking and eating berries. The berries were so good they decided to pick them again in the morning so they could have raspberry pancakes and blueberry muffins.

It had been a long, hard day for both of them, and by nine o'clock, they were in their sleeping bags, ready for bed. They lay in their tent and talked for a while, but when the full moon came up around nine-thirty, they were both asleep. They didn't know they had a neighbor less than a quarter of a mile east of them on Gogebic Lake. And they didn't know that someone else would be at their campsite before the night was over.

After dinner, Dick leaned against a tree and looked out on the lake. He really enjoyed this time of day, just before it got dark. He could see the last few rays of sunshine barely touching the tops of the tallest pine trees. And in front of him a mirrored image of the lake was cast upon the smooth surface of the lake. The opposite shoreline was almost completely dark. There was no wind, just the tranquil silence of the forest. This was known to many campers as the witching hour.

Dick strained to hear even the most subtle sounds, like crickets chirping, fish feeding on the surface, or water lapping on the shore. His campfire had gone out, and as he sat in the growing darkness, he was almost mesmerized by the stillness around him.

Then he heard something that scared the living daylights out of him.

From across the lake came the sound of an aluminum canoe scraping the gravel shoreline. Someone else had come to Gogebic.

Dick quickly grabbed his binoculars, stretched out on his stomach, and strained to see across the lake. For a while, he couldn't see anything because it was so dark along the shoreline. Then, out of the darkness, he saw two men paddling a canoe toward the west end of the lake.

At first he thought they were the two men Bransky had sent after him, but these two were smaller and moved more gracefully. Each man wore a western-style hat with a single feather in the brim. As the canoe moved farther away from shore, Dick could see a hunting bow and quiver of arrows braced against the portage yoke.

The smaller of the two men sat motionless in the front. The man in back guided the canoe noiselessly across the water. Then they eased into the shadows and disappeared. They were obviously going somewhere beyond the lake, but Dick couldn't see where.

Dick thought the two men must be poachers. He couldn't see any other reason why they would be there so late at night with a hunting bow. He wanted to walk along the trail to the west end of the lake to see what they were up to, but then he thought he'd better not. He knew that many poachers could kill a man as easily as they could kill a deer. And if he surprised them while they were in the act of taking game illegally, they just might put an arrow through him.

Dick untied the support rope and let his tent drop so it wouldn't be seen. He thought of moving his canoe, which was on shore and turned over, but he was afraid that any sound he made would carry across the lake and be heard by the poachers. He waited and listened for sounds to come from the west end of the lake, but there was only the quite stillness of the forest that he had been enjoying minutes earlier.

A half hour later the moon came up and cast an erie glow across the entire lake. Dick could see better now, but the shoreline was still clothed in darkness. He was straining to see the far end of the lake when he saw the two men again.

They moved steadily and quietly down the lake just as they had earlier. The man in back paddled while the one in front sat hunched over. The bow and quiver were still leaned against the portage yoke. Dick watched them move back to the place where the trail came up from West Pike.

Then the man in front said something that Dick couldn't hear. Suddenly they stopped. The man in back gently touched the shoulder of the one in front with his canoe paddle and they both looked across the lake in Dick's direction. Dick felt like his heart was in his throat as the two men continued to stare right at him. The man in back held the canoe perfectly still for what seemed to Dick to be an eternity. Then the man turned and paddled the canoe to shore, and they were lost again in the shadows. Dick listened for the sound of the canoe scraping bottom, but he didn't hear a thing.

Dick wondered how the two men could've brought a canoe up the trail from West Pike without making any noise. When he came up, he hardly missed a tree. The banging of aluminum against trees made an awful racket, but now he heard nothing.

Then Dick was afraid the men might not have gone and were still on the other shore. Either that, or they'd started walking along the shoreline toward him.

To be safe, Dick thought he'd better move. He got up and quietly walked toward the east end of the lake. If the two men came around that way, they'd have to climb over the beaver dam to get to him. And if they did, they'd be where he could see and hear them.

When Dick got to the east end of the lake, he waited in the old campground to see what would happen. He leaned against a tree and trained his binoculars on the north shore. No one was there. The two men, whoever they were, had left Gogebic Lake as quietly as they'd arrived.

When he was sure that the two men had gone, Dick went back to his campsite. He put up his tent, crawled in, and got ready for bed. He was still puzzled over what he'd seen and decided that the first thing he'd do in the morning would be to find out what had gone on at the west end of the lake. Then he got into his sleeping bag and fell asleep. The night was not going to end that peacefully, however.

At the same time Dick was watching the two men on Gogebic, a dark van pulled into an abandoned cabin site at the west end of Clearwater. It moved quietly through the trees, past an unfinished cabin, and down to the lakeshore where it stopped. A man got out and lifted a square-stern, fiberglass canoe from the cartop carrier. He took the canoe to the lake and set it in the water next to an unfinished dock. Then he went back to the van, got a battery-powered outboard motor, and attached it to the rear of his canoe. To cut down on noise, he covered the motor with a styrofoam cover. He made one more trip to the van and got a flashlight, a hunting bow, and a quiver of arrows. Within minutes he was quietly on his way toward the east end of Clearwater.

Forty minutes later the man guided his canoe into a shallow cove between the 250-foot palisade and the West Pike portage. He headed across the cove to a point on the south shore near a fallen pine tree. Then he beached his canoe and pulled it up into the trees where it couldn't be seen.

The man picked up his bow, quiver of arrows, and flashlight and moved quickly up a narrow, winding trail. He continued to climb until he reached the Border Route Trail where it came south from the Clearwater-West Pike portage. Then he turned north for another ten yards until he came to a deer trail that led through an aspen grove to a small clearing. He walked along the north side of the clearing until he reached a fallen spruce tree at the edge of a small pond. There, beneath several freshly cut cedar boughs, he found two large backpacks.

The packs, which had been left there earlier in the day by two French Canadians, contained narcotics and other contraband. The man who was there to pick them up was part of a smuggling ring that had been operating back and forth across the Canadian border for almost five years. He planned to make two trips to carry the heavy packs down the trail to the cove. Then he'd load them in his canoe, return to his van, and drive back to Grand Marais.

The man grunted as he picked up one of the heavy packs and swung it to his back. He left the other pack for his next trip and headed back down the trail to his canoe.

Lisa woke suddenly and thought she'd heard a bear. She lay quietly in her sleeping bag and listened for another sound. Then she heard what sounded like a large animal moving through the woods. She got out of her sleeping bag and put on her Levis, sweatshirt, and boots. As she was doing so, she woke Judy.

"What are you doing?" asked Judy.

"There's a bear out there," said Lisa.

"Well leave it alone and it'll go away."

"If I hear it again, I'm going out there and take a picture of it."

"Go to sleep and forget the picture."

"I'm going to use my flash," said Lisa. "I'll get a picture and scare the bear at the same time."

By now, Judy was wide awake. "I don't hear anything," she said.

"I don't either," said Lisa, "but I did. I'm going out for a picture as soon as it comes back."

"You can sit up and wait if you want to, but I'm going back to sleep."

Judy pulled her sleeping bag over her head and turned toward the side of the tent. Lisa lay on her back with her camera in her hand and listened for the return of the bear.

A half hour later, as she was about to go to sleep again, Lisa heard something moving around outside. She shook Judy and woke her up.

"The bear is back," whispered Lisa. "Come on, let's take a picture."

"You're crazy, Lisa. Go back to sleep."

"Listen" said Lisa. "Did you hear that? Something is out there." She grabbed her camera and crawled quickly out of the tent.

On the north side of the clearing, the man stopped suddenly and listened. He thought he heard a noise to his right at the other edge of the clearing. He waited until he heard the noise again. Then he dropped to his knees and carefully strung an arrow. Something was coming toward him.

Lisa stopped about ten feet in front of the tent and whispered back to Judy. "Come on, but be quiet. I think it's over at the edge of the clearing."

Judy quickly got out of her sleeping bag and put on her clothes. She was out of the tent in a minute. If Lisa scared a bear, it could come after them, and Judy didn't want to be caught in the tent if it did.

The full moon shone through the tall pine trees and gave an erie glow to the landscape. Judy could just barely see Lisa in the clearing ahead of her.

The man was ready with his bow and arrow, but he needed to get in a better position if he had to shoot whatever it was that was coming toward him. He slowly raised to one knee, and as he did, a twig snapped beneath his foot. The sound was not very loud, but both Lisa and the man heard it.

Lisa kept moving quietly toward the edge of the clearing as the man drew back his bowstring. Then, as Lisa aimed her camera toward a fallen spruce tree, the man aimed his arrow at the shadowy figure that stood less than fifty feet away in the center of the clearing.

Suddenly, for a fraction of a second, the flash of Lisa's camera lit up the entire clearing. The man instinctively released his arrow, sending it straight across the clearing and right through Lisa's chest. Judy saw the man shoot Lisa when the flash went off, and she screamed as she heard the arrow hit Lisa's body. Then she turned from the corner of the tent where she'd been standing and ran down the trail behind her.

The man knew right away from the scream he heard that he'd hit someone. It sounded like it came from a woman. But he wasn't sure, because he'd shot at the flash and couldn't see anything else. Now he waited to see who was out there. He heard someone crashing through the woods beyond the clearing, and then it was quiet.

The man sat motionless in the moonlight and waited a few minutes more. Then he strung another arrow and held it against the bow in his left hand. With his flashlight in his right hand, he stood up and slowly moved out into the clearing.

He snapped on the light and shined it out in front of him. He couldn't see anybody, but he saw a tent at the other end of the clearing and very quietly walked toward it. About halfway there he found Lisa's body lying on the ground with an arrow sticking out of her chest. He dropped down beside her and saw that she was dead. Then he carefully moved over to the tent and shined his light inside. It was obvious that two people had been using it, so he figured someone else must have seen him when the flash went off. That person was probably hiding somewhere in the woods.

The man felt bad that he'd killed the woman, but at the same time, he felt it couldn't be helped. He knew something like this might happen when he started coming out here. He also knew he'd have to find, and probably kill, the other person who was hiding from him. But he couldn't do it now, because he was running out of time. He had to take the packs to Grand Marais, process the contents, and get them ready for an early morning pickup.

He went back to Lisa's body and decided to hide it in the woods. If no one could find it right away, the search would have to be extended. That would give him more time to come back and take care of the dead woman's companion.

He slung his bow and quiver over his shoulder and picked up the body. He carried it through the aspen grove and down the trail toward his canoe. After going several yards, he moved off the trail and placed the body near a fallen tree. He covered it with cedar boughs and other debris, and then went back to the clearing.

The man looked in the tent again and in the wooded area next to the clearing, but he still couldn't see or hear anyone. He knew the area was not a designated Forest Service campsite, so he didn't expect anyone else to come by. He also knew that whoever was hiding in the woods was probably frightened enough to be out there for a long time.

The man came back to the clearing and looked around again. He suspected the flash he'd seen had come from a camera, so he spent a few minutes looking for it. When he couldn't find it, he thought it must have been thrown aside when the woman was hit. He knew he'd have to come back and look for that too, especially if his picture was on the film. But right now he had to get out of there. He was running out of time.

He went back to the north edge of the clearing and picked up the second pack. Then he hurried down the trail to his canoe and was gone.

Judy ran as fast as she could down the deer trail that entered the woods from the south side of the clearing. She fell several times in the darkness, but she got back up again and kept running. Then, in the moonlight, she saw a large, uprooted pine tree and crawled under it. The branches scratched her skin and tore at her clothes, but she was well hidden. The tree had fallen into a boggy area, so the ground beneath her was cold and damp. That didn't bother her, she just wanted to hide.

Judy cried softly to herself as she thought about Lisa. She didn't know what happened to her, and she was too scared to go back to the clearing to find out. She had seen the man shoot an arrow at Lisa and heard it hit, but she didn't know what had happened after that. Now she was afraid the man was coming after her. She was cold and wet and afraid to move. She prayed that she wouldn't be seen.

Judy started to fall asleep several times during the night. Then she'd think she heard something and she'd be awake again. Finally, about an hour before dawn, she fell into a deep sleep.

WEDNESDAY

Dick crawled out of his tent as the sun came up. He took a quick bath, built a good-sized fire, and cooked breakfast.

As he sat drinking his hot chocolate, he thought about the two men he'd seen the night before. He was curious to know who they were and what they were doing at the west end of the lake. He decided to spend the first part of the morning trying to find some answers.

After he cleaned his cooking utensils and stowed them under his overturned canoe, he started down the narrow deer trail that ran along the south side of the lake. The trail continued to the west end and then branched off. One route continued straight ahead through the woods, the other curved to the right and followed the shoreline through a marshy area along the west end of the lake. He stayed on the trail that took him through the marsh.

Dick walked across rocks and fallen trees to the north side of the lake where the trail ended abruptly against a sheer rock wall. The wall extended all along the north shore to the point where the two strangers had put in their canoes. Dick tried to sort out all the game trails that headed into the marsh, but he couldn't see one that was any different than the others.

He walked back across the marsh to the place where the trail had divided. Then he turned and headed west past several blueberry bushes into a raspberry patch. He was happy to see all the berries, but he was bothered by all the animal tracks. He was obviously in bear country.

Dick stayed on the trail past the berry patch. Then he heard a noise that stopped him cold. Something had moved ahead and to his left near a fallen pine tree. He stood motionless and listened carefully, but the woods were silent. He didn't know if he had startled a bear or was about to encounter a moose, and he sure didn't want to meet up with either one of them on a narrow trail like this.

He started to walk again when suddenly, a young woman jumped out from behind the fallen tree. She looked at Dick, screamed, and started running down the trail. Dick was so startled he almost fell over. When he saw it was a young woman, he called out to her as he ran behind her down the trail.

"Wait! Don't run," he shouted.

But she ran on, leaping over fallen branches and trying to stay on the trail. Then she fell, and before she could get up, Dick had overtaken her.

When he reached out to help her, she screamed and tried to hit him. Her face was a mask of terror as he fended off her blows, grabbed her arms, and held on to her.

"Hey, calm down," he said. "I'm not going to hurt you. It's okay."

Judy stopped struggling then and started to sob. Dick held her close and tried to assure her that everything was all right. She felt cold against his body, which made him think she must have spent the night in the woods.

"I'm Dick Christopher," he said. "Do you want to tell me what's going on?"

Judy tried to talk between sobs as she stood up to face Dick.

"I'm Judy . . . Miller . . . My friend and I . . . were camping here . . . last night and . . . " She started crying again.

Dick reached out for her again, but she shook her head and said, "No . . . please . . . I'll be all right."

Dick gave her some time to pull herself together. "You've got a friend out here?" he asked.

"I think she's dead," said Judy. "We were asleep in our tent when we heard noises. Lisa thought a bear was outside. She wanted to get a picture of it and scare it off with her flash camera." Judy was trying hard not to cry again.

Dick waited until she was ready to go on with her story.

"It wasn't a bear," she said. "It was a man with a bow and arrow. When the flash went off, he shot an arrow right at her. I heard it hit her, and now she's dead. I know she's dead."

Judy fell to her knees and started sobbing again. Dick helped her back to her feet, held her close, and tried to comfort her. She was cold, wet, and very frightened. Her arms and face were covered with scratches, and her clothes were torn and dirty.

Dick immediately thought about the two men he'd seen the night before. He remembered seeing a bow and quiver of arrows in their canoe.

Judy again said she was all right and stepped back from Dick.

"Did you see what the man looked like?" asked Dick.

"No, I didn't. It was too dark."

"Where are you camped?"

"Back there," said Judy as she pointed toward the woods behind her. "There's a clearing back there next to a little pond. It's not a designated campsite."

"How did you get in there?" asked Dick. "I had a helluva time getting to where I am."

"We came up the Border Route Trail from the Clearwater-West Pike portage. We found the clearing by accident and decided to stay there."

"Where did you see the man with the bow and arrow?"

"He was at the north edge of the clearing. Our tent is at the south edge. That's where I was, next to the tent. Lisa was walking toward him in the middle of the clearing when he shot her. I ran away and hid under that pine tree over there. I didn't hear or see anything after that, and I was too frightened to go back and find out what happened."

"I'll go over there now and look around," said Dick. "You stay here until I get back."

Judy wanted to go along, but Dick told her it would be better if she stayed right where she was. He walked down the trail, stopped at the edge of the clearing, and looked over the entire area. He saw the tent, and it appeared to be undisturbed. Then he looked across at the other side of the clearing where Judy said the killer had been. He walked slowly across the clearing to the aspen grove. No one was there, and there was no body.

Dick found a path at the aspen grove and followed it until he came to what he assumed was the Border Route Trail. He looked around again and then went back through the aspen grove, crossed the clearing, and returned to the place where he'd left Judy. She looked up when she heard him coming.

"I couldn't find her," he said.

"What do you mean?"

"There was no body. Whoever shot her must have carried her away."

"Oh no," said Judy as she started crying again.

"Come on," said Dick as he put his arm around her. "Let's go over to my tent. I'll get you some warm clothes and something to eat."

When Dick and Judy got back to his campsite on Gogebic, he took a wool sweater out of his pack and helped her put it on. After he added several pieces of beaver wood to his fire, he had her sit close to it so she could get warm. Then he fixed her a cup of hot chocolate and gave her some blueberry biscuits.

Judy sat by the fire and drank the hot chocolate, but she could only eat a few bites of the biscuits. She was still very upset and didn't think she could keep much of anything on her stomach. As soon as Dick saw she was feeling better, he started asking her questions about what had happened the night before. Judy repeated her story about how Lisa had been shot. She still found it hard to believe that Lisa's body was not in the clearing.

"I looked all over," said Dick, "but I couldn't find her anywhere. I walked down to the Border Route Trail and back, but there wasn't anything there either. She might not even be dead. She might have been badly hurt and gone for help. Or the person who shot her might have taken her somewhere. I just don't know what happened to her."

Judy sat quietly and tried to muffle another sob.

"I think I'd better get the sheriff out here right away," said Dick.

"How are you going to do that?"

"I'll have to go for help," he said as he got out his trail map. "Is this where you came up from the portage?"

"The Trail crosses the portage right there," said Judy as she pointed to the map.

"I'll go down to Clearwater and see if I can find someone who'll go up to Nelson's Lodge. They can call the sheriff from there."

"I'd like to go back to my tent," said Judy. "I need some things."

"Do you think you should?"

"I'm all right. I have to be. I have to find Lisa."

The two of them walked back over the trail to the clearing.

"You'd better not move things around too much," said Dick. "The sheriff will probably want to look for clues or prints or something. If it's too uncomfortable for you here, you can go back over to my tent."

"I'll just get some clean clothes," said Judy. "Then I think I will go back to your tent. I still need to get warm."

"Okay," said Dick, "I'll be back as soon as I can."

Dick hurried down the Border Route Trail until he came to the Clearwater-West Pike portage. Then he turned toward Clearwater and ran along the portage until he came to the landing. He was in luck. A group of three canoes was coming in from about a half mile out on the lake. When they got close to shore, he could see from the emblem on the canoes that they were from the YMCA camp on West Bearskin. The group was made up of eight young boys and a counselor who appeared to be in his twenties. As they brought their canoes ashore, Dick introduced himself to the counselor.

"Hello, I'm Dick Christopher. Are you from Camp Menogyn?"

"Yes," said Alex Craig. "We're out on a shakedown cruise."

"I need some help," said Dick. "Can we talk privately?"

"Sure," said Alex. Then he turned to his campers. "You guys wait here by the canoes. I'll be right back."

Dick and Alex walked down the portage until they were out of earshot of the boys.

"What's up?" asked Alex.

"A young woman was murdered out here last night," said Dick. "I need to get word to the sheriff."

"Wow! Where did it happen?"

"Up on the Border Route Trail just south of here. Could you take one of your canoes and go back up Clearwater to Nelson's Lodge? You can place a call from there."

"I can do better than that," said Alex. "I've got a CB radio in my pack. I'll call Menogyn and have them get in touch with the sheriff right away."

"I don't think you should tell your campers," said Dick. "I'd just as soon keep this quiet until after the sheriff gets out here."

"That's no problem. I'll have them move on to West Pike."

They turned and went back to the campers. Alex had two of the boys take canoes while the others gathered up the packs, fishing tackle, and paddles.

"You guys trade off with the canoes at each of the rest stops," said Alex. "Wait for me when you get to West Pike. I'll bring the other canoe as soon as I can. Now get moving."

Alex called Camp Menogyn as soon as the boys were gone. The camp director took the call in his office and assured Alex that he'd contact the sheriff right away. After asking Alex for directions on how to get to the clearing, he signed off and put in a call to the sheriff.

"Are you guys going to spend a lot of time on West Pike?" asked Dick.

"No," said Alex. "We'll just be passing through. We're heading for the far end of East Pike where we'll stop for lunch and do some fishing. We're only going to be out for the day, so we'll be coming back through here before it gets dark."

"Then I'd like you to do me another favor," said Dick.

"Sure, whatever you need."

"Two men are on the island in West Pike without a canoe. I set their's adrift yesterday, and I expect it's probably beached somewhere along the north or east shore of the lake."

"Boy, you're really a nice guy."

"They're the kind of men you want to stay away from. I don't think they're involved in what happened here last night, but they could still cause some trouble. I think it'd be good for them if they spent another day on the island."

"What do you want us to do?"

"Swing clear of them when you go down the lake, but see if you can find their canoe. Then when you come back tonight, give it back to them. I think they'll be ready to get out of here by then. They may not leave tonight, but I'm sure they'll take off first thing in the morning."

"We'll do it," said Alex. "But won't they come looking for you?"

"They don't know where I am. And after what happened here last night, I'm sure I won't be around here much longer anyway."

"Do you know who did the killing?" asked Alex.

"No, I don't, but hopefully it'll all get straightened out when the sheriff gets here."

"Well," said Alex, "I'd better hustle now and catch up with my troops. I won't tell them what's going on until we're well away from here. And I'll keep close to the north shore of West Pike so we stay away from your friends."

"Thanks," said Dick. "And thanks for the use of your radio."

Dick waited while Alex picked up the remaining canoe. Then the two of them headed down the portage toward West Pike. When they reached the Border Route Trail, Dick said goodbye and started back to his campsite. A light rain began to fall as he went up the Trail.

Sheriff Barney Ross was in Emma's Cafe when he got a call to come back to his office. He gave Emma a dollar for a roll and a cup of coffee, gulped down what was left, and hurried out the door to his Chevy Blazer. His secretary, Maggie McCabe, had standing orders not to bother him when he went to Emma's for coffee or lunch unless it was really important. So in anticipation of a serious incident, he started getting butterflies in his stomach as he sped up to the Court House.

"What's up, Maggie?" he asked as he came through the door of his office.

"I'm not sure," said Maggie. "We got this report third-hand from the camp director at Menogyn. He got it from one of his counselors who radioed in from Clearwater. Some guy out there told the counselor that a young woman had been killed on the Border Route Trail."

"Killed? How?"

"She was murdered."

"Holy cow!" exclaimed Barney. "Up on the Border Route Trail?"

"That's what he said. The counselor was taking a group of campers from Clearwater to West Pike when he met this guy at the Clearwater end of the portage. The woman was apparently killed on the Trail right south of Clearwater."

"Who's the guy who told the counselor?"

"The director didn't say. I suppose he was a camper."

"Well I'd better get out there and see what's going on," said Barney. "Where are Maynard and Don?"

"Maynard is serving an eviction notice over by Hoveland and Don is checking out a burglary at Lutsen."

"You'd better get them both on the radio and tell them what happened. And you'd better call Doc Martin and tell him to put on his coroner's hat. I don't think we'll need Maynard or Don right away, but I know we'll need Doc. When I find out what happened out there I'll call you. Do we have a helicopter in the area?"

"No," said Maggie, "it's in Duluth today. The Forest Service said they'd have it back here tomorrow."

"Then I'll have to take the boat down Clearwater and hike up the Trail. I'll see you later."

Barney left the basement office and backed his Blazer into the county garage. His seventeen-foot boat and ten-horsepower outboard motor were attached to a trailer and ready to go. He checked the gas tank and hitched the trailer to the Blazer. Then he left the garage and headed up the Gunflint Trail toward Clearwater Lake.

As soon as Barney cleared the top of Lookout Hill, he ran into a heavy rainstorm. The sky to the north and west told him it would be raining for quite a while.

"Damn," thought Barney. "This is really going to be a mess. I'm going to get soaked clear through if this rain keeps up."

As he drove along the blacktop, he wondered what he'd see when he got to the murder scene. He still didn't know who'd been killed, or how it'd been done.

"Why would anyone want to go and kill somebody up here?" he asked himself.

Then Barney thought about the sheriff's workshop he'd attended two years ago in St. Paul. One of the sessions dealt with the investigation and handling of murder cases. He took good notes and listened carefully as each speaker talked about investigative procedures. But there had only been two murders in over thirty years in Cook County. So at the time, he didn't see how he'd ever apply the things he heard. Now he was trying to remember everything that was said.

"Clues," he said aloud. "I've got to look for clues. But how in hell am I going to find any clues if it keeps raining like this."

Barney thought back over the six years that he'd been sheriff in Cook County. And he thought about the years before that when he was in Viet Nam and then a member of the Hibbing and Grand Marais police departments. At twenty-eight, he'd been one of the youngest sheriffs in the state when he was elected. The job had been exciting for him when he started, but it had lost something over the years. Either that, or he had. Now he spent most of his time working on burglaries, catching speeders, and arresting game-law violators. It really bothered him to have to go out and recover a drowning victim from one of the hundreds of lakes in the county. But other than the drownings, there wasn't much reason for Maggie to call him out of Emma's Cafe.

Barney was thinking so much about the pending investigation that he almost missed the turnoff to Clearwater. He turned down the gravel road and sped toward Nelson's Lodge. He wanted to put the boat in there instead of the public landing, because Sue Nelson had a phone he could use if he had to. And besides, he wanted to stop and say hello.

When Barney got to Nelson's, he drove down to the dock, turned around, and backed the boat trailer into the water. He put on his waterproof pants and parka, got out of the Blazer, and unhitched the boat from the trailer. He eased the boat into the water, rowed it over to the dock, and tied it up. When he got back in the Blazer, he could see Sue standing on the porch of the main lodge. He waved to her as he drove past on his way to the parking lot. Then he grabbed his day pack with his two-way radio and his service revolver and hurried to the porch as the rain continued to fall.

"Hello, Barney," said Sue. "What brings you out here on such a nice day? You can't be going fishing."

"No, I'm afraid not, Sue. This time I'm here on business. We heard there was a killing on the Border Route Trail south of Clearwater."

"A killing? Do you mean a camper?"

"That's what we heard," said Barney. "Some man stopped a group from Menogyn and asked them to call for help."

Sue thought immediately of Dick. "Oh my goodness," she said, "I hope it's not one of my people."

"Have you got a camper out there who might be involved?"

"I hope not, but he could be." Then Sue told Barney about Dick and the two men who were following him.

"Did you see these two men?"

"No, I didn't. But from what Dick said, they're big and mean. They stopped by here on Monday and tried to find out where Dick was. I sure hope he's not involved in anything like a killing."

"Well it won't do any good to worry about it," said Barney. "I'll stop back here as soon as I can and let you know what happened."

Barney didn't think he'd have any trouble with the men who were chasing Dick. If he ran into them, he figured he could handle them. He wasn't quite six feet tall, but he weighed a solid 190 pounds. The exercising and weight lifting he did allowed him to hold his own with any man.

As Barney thought about the two men, he wondered if they were the same ones who left the mess at the Flour Lake Campground Monday night.

Barney thanked Sue for the use of her dock, said goodbye, and went down to his boat. He borrowed a dry seat cushion from Sue's boathouse and put it in his boat. Then he got in, shoved off, and started the motor. It was still raining hard as he swung the boat around and headed for the east end of the lake.

———

Judy was trying to stay warm and dry as she rested in Dick's tent. Dick was sitting on a log under a tarpaulin he'd rigged up between two trees. He was drinking a cup of coffee and trying to make sense out of what happened to Lisa and Judy. He kept thinking about the two men he'd seen on Gogebic the night before. They had a bow and quiver of arrows, but they were in and out before Lisa was killed, unless Judy was confused about the time it happened.

The two men could also have gone back to the clearing after Dick saw them. They still seemed to him to be logical suspects. After all, he thought, there couldn't be a whole helluva lot of people going around the north woods in the middle of the night with bows and arrows.

He thought they were probably poaching. And when Lisa surprised them with her flash camera, one of them panicked and shot her. But he still couldn't figure out why Lisa's body had been moved. He thought if the two men had taken it, he would've seen them carry it out when they left Gogebic.

The whole episode seemed very unreal to Dick. He came to the BWCA to work out problems he was having with Bransky. And now he was faced with another, even more important, predicament. He wished he could come up with some answers pretty soon, not only about the murder, but for his own concerns as well.

The rain showed no sign of letting up. And even though he didn't want to go out in it again, he thought he'd better go down to Clearwater and wait for the sheriff. If calls went through like they were supposed to, the sheriff would probably be arriving at the portage pretty soon.

Dick stuck his head inside the tent and saw that Judy was asleep. When he touched her arm to wake her, she jumped up with a frightened look on her face.

"Hey," said Dick, "it's okay. It's me."

"I'm sorry," said Judy. "I was dreaming about last night. You scared me."

"Well you're going to be all right, so don't worry. I'm leaving now to go down to Clearwater and wait for the sheriff. I'll be back as soon as he gets here."

"Let me come with you," said Judy. "I'm still scared."

"Okay, if you want to. But it's still raining pretty hard, so you'd better put on your rain poncho."

Dick closed the tent and went back under the tarpaulin to wait for Judy. When she was ready, they stepped out in the rain and headed for Clearwater.

When they got to the clearing, Dick asked Judy if she could remember where she and Lisa had been standing when Lisa got shot.

"I think Lisa was standing over there," said Judy. "When we heard the noise, Lisa got out of the tent and walked straight ahead. I stayed over here by the side of the tent. The man who killed her was over there somewhere," she said as she pointed to the north edge of the clearing.

"The rain must have washed all the blood away," said Dick. "I can't see any now."

"Why did he carry her away?" asked Judy as tears came to her eyes.

"I don't know," said Dick. "But don't worry, we'll find her. Now come on, we'd better get down to Clearwater."

Dick and Judy followed the trail through the aspen grove over to the Border Route Trail. Then, with the palisade to their left, they hiked down to the Clearwater-West Pike portage. When they got to the bottom of the hill, they turned west toward Clearwater. They could hear the whine of an outboard motor in the distance and assumed it was the sheriff. He was still a mile away when they reached the lake.

Barney saw a man and woman in rain gear waiting for him as he neared the Clearwater-West Pike portage. The man met his boat as he came in and pulled it ashore.

"Hello," said Dick, "are you the sheriff?"

"Yes, I'm Sheriff Barney Ross. Who are you?"

"I'm Dick Christopher, and this is Judy Miller. I'm the one who put in the call to you."

"What's going on?" asked Barney as he got out of his boat. "We heard there was a killing out here."

"My friend Lisa was killed last night," said Judy. "Someone shot her with a bow and arrow."

"A bow and arrow? That's unusual," said Barney. "She must have run into some poachers."

"We thought we heard a bear outside our tent, so Lisa got her camera and went to scare it away."

"With a camera?" asked Barney.

"It's a flash camera. Lisa thought the flash would frighten it. But when she took the picture, a man shot her with a bow and arrow. He was just sitting there ready to shoot when the flash went off." Tears came to Judy's eyes as she told the sheriff about Lisa's death.

"It sure sounds like a poacher," said Barney. "I don't know who else would be out in the woods with a bow and arrow in the middle of the night." Then he turned to Dick. "Sue Nelson says two men are out here chasing after you. Do you think they're mixed up in this?"

"No," said Dick. "I really don't think so. They don't know what they're doing out here. And besides, they're stranded on an island over in West Pike. But I did see two other men who could be the ones you're looking for."

"Who are they?"

Dick told Barney about the two men who'd come and gone during the night on Gogebic.

"Did you get a good look at them?" asked Barney.

"Not really," said Dick. "They stayed in the shadows along the shoreline. It was pretty dark when they came back, even though the moon was up then. They sure were quiet."

"You said there were two of them. Was one smaller and older than the other? Kind of bent over?"

"Yes," said Dick. "I remember that."

"Were they both wearing western hats? With feathers?"

"Yes, they were."

"Damn," said Barney. "It sounds like Red Hawk and his uncle."

"Do you know them?" asked Dick.

"Yes, I do. They're a couple of Indians who live in a cabin over on Hungry Jack Lake. The tall one is Red Hawk. He was an all-around athlete in high school and a good football player at the University of Minnesota. He got drafted into the Army, went to Viet Nam, and had an outstanding service record. Helluva good man.

"His uncle's name is Running Deer. There's not much to say about him.

"After Hawk got back from Viet Nam, he moved to Minneapolis, went to law school, and worked parttime. Then one night about five years ago, his folks got to drinking with his uncle. When they were all pretty well loaded, Hawk's uncle went outside and got sick. Something caught fire inside the house and it burned down before Hawk's folks could get out. They couldn't find enough of either one of them to bury them, so they scooped up the whole mess and dumped it in a landfill. It just about killed Hawk.

"He quit school, came back up here, and moved in with his uncle. The two of them hire out as hunting and fishing guides, and that's about it. I think they do a lot of poaching around here, but I've never been able to catch them at it."

"Do you think one of them killed Lisa?" asked Judy.

"Well," said Barney, "if they were out here last night with a bow and arrow, and that's how your friend got killed, then I'd have to think one of them did it. They could've panicked when the two of you came out of your tent, not knowing who or what was coming at them. Or they might have thought Lisa was a deer and were already to shoot when the flash went off. It must have scared the daylights out of both of them. It's just too bad that they ended up shooting your friend.

"And now we'd better get up to your camp site. I'm getting tired of standing around in this god-awful rain. Then I'll have to call the coroner right away and have him come out as soon as he's finished in surgery to examine the body."

"We might have a problem with that," said Dick.

"What do you mean?" asked Barney.

"The killer, or killers, apparently carried off Lisa's body. We can't find her anywhere."

"Come on," said Barney, "you can tell me about it along the way."

The three of them went down the portage to the Border Route Trail and then hiked to the clearing. Judy told Barney everything she could remember about the night before. Dick told him about his first look at the clearing and how he missed seeing Lisa's body. Both Dick and Judy talked about the camera and of their inability to find it.

"Did you touch anything?" asked Barney as they walked into the clearing.

"I went to our tent over there and got some clothes and things," said Judy. "But that's all."

"Was anything missing from your tent?"

"Not that I could see," said Judy.

"Where was your friend when she was hit?" asked Barney.

"I think she was right over here," said Judy as she walked to the center of the clearing. "But it was dark. I just can't be sure."

The three of them walked all over the area for the next half hour while they looked for the camera and anything else that might provide some clues.

"Why would anyone want to take Lisa's body?" asked Judy as she turned to Barney.

"I don't know," said Barney. "That's hard to figure out. Did they chase after you?"

"I was so scared, I just ran. I don't know if anyone was behind me or not. I crawled under a fallen pine tree and stayed there all night. I didn't see or hear anything until Dick found me this morning."

Then Barney turned to Dick. "Did you say you saw the two men come back out of this area and leave through Gogebic?"

"Yes," said Dick, "but it was pretty dark when I saw them the second time through my binoculars. They might have seen me, but I can't be sure. They stayed real close to shore, and when they got to the trail that goes back to West Pike, I lost them in the shadows."

"Were they carrying anything?"

"Nothing that I could see. But like I said, it was pretty dark."

"When we get done here," said Barney, "we'd better go over to Gogebic and look around."

They continued their search for Lisa's body and the camera. Then Dick called over to Barney from the north edge of the clearing.

"Sheriff, look at this. There's a trail over here, and it looks like it was used recently."

"Yes it does," said Barney. "It looks like it goes over to Gogebic. Did you come this way?"

"No," said Dick, "we came along the south edge of the pond."

Barney and Dick walked along the trail until they got to the west shore of Gogebic.

"This is probably the way the two Indians came in," said Barney.

"I'm sure of it," said Dick. "I was down at the other end of the lake and could see them coming out on the water right about here. And look, someone pulled a canoe up on the grass over here. I walked by here this morning and completely missed this trail."

"You wouldn't have seen it unless you knew it was here," said Barney. "There are lots of game trails over here, and all this rain isn't making it any easier to see much of anything. Come on, let's go back to the clearing."

Barney and Dick went back to where Judy was still searching.

"We're not going to get much done out here today," said Barney, "so let's all go back to town. The weather is supposed to clear tonight. Then we can come back tomorrow morning with some more people and try to find Lisa's body. It'll also give me a chance to find Red Hawk and his uncle and bring them in for questioning."

"I can't go back," said Judy. "Not until I find Lisa."

"Well you won't find her now," said Barney. "It's too hard to do much of anything when it's raining this hard, especially when you don't even know where to look. A couple of men in town have good trail dogs. We can use them just as soon as the weather clears."

"I still want to stay."

"Well suit yourself. How about you, Dick?"

"I'll stay too. The rain might let up enough for us to do some more looking before dark, and I sure don't want to leave Judy out here by herself. But how can we get in touch with you again if we do find Lisa?"

"I'll leave my radio with you. You can call Camp Menogyn like you did before, and they can get word to me right away."

"Sheriff," asked Judy, "do you think it's safe out here? Will those men come back?"

"I don't know, Judy. Poachers can be awful desperate if they think they're going to get caught. If they killed Lisa, they may come after you too. You'd better move over to Gogebic and stay with Dick tonight. But leave your tent and everything here as it is. We'll want to go over it in the morning."

Then Barney got his radio out of his day pack and called Camp Menogyn.

"Chip? This is Sheriff Ross. Can you hear me all right?"

"Barney? This is Chip. Where are you?"

"I'm on the Border Route Trail south of Clearwater where the young woman was killed last night. I'm leaving two people here tonight until I can get some more help. They may have to call on you again if they run into anymore trouble."

"Do you need help from us?" asked Chip. "We've got lots of people here."

"I don't think so, Chip. But thanks for the offer. If we come up short, I'll get back to you."

"Is the man who called in this morning with you now?" asked Chip.

"Yes, he is."

"Tell him our boys found the canoe that belongs to the two men on West Pike Island."

Barney turned to Dick and asked, "What's that all about?"

"Tell him they can have their canoe back," said Dick. "I'll fill you in when you're done talking."

"Chip, he says to give them back their canoe. And Chip, would you please call the hospital and tell Doc Martin he won't have to come out yet? Keep the line open. We'll talk to you again tomorrow."

After Barney signed off, Dick told him how he stranded Bruno and Chet on the island.

"What happens after they get their canoe?" asked Barney.

"After being stuck on that island for two days in all this rain, I'd guess they'll be ready to get back to Minneapolis."

"We sure don't need those two up here," said Barney.

"I doubt if they'll come," said Dick. "I think they'll hightail it for home as soon as they can. Besides, they're not too smart. I doubt if they could find their way up here anyway."

"Just be careful," said Barney. "I'll see you two in the morning."

After they said goodbye, Barney headed back to town, and Dick and Judy went back to the campsite on Gogebic. The rain continued to fall.

Barney left his boat and trailer at Nelson's Lodge and drove back to Grand Marais. As he headed down the Trail, he thought about clues and knew he didn't have very many. There were several things he couldn't figure out. It looked like Hawk and his uncle could've been involved in the killing, but he wasn't completely sure. He wasn't even sure that Lisa was dead, and he couldn't be sure until he found her body. She may have crawled away on her own, or the killer might have taken her somewhere. He was guessing, and it frustrated him.

Barney planned to go back to the clearing early the next morning with his two deputies. He also wanted to bring someone along who had a good dog and was good at tracking. The first person he thought of was Lester Malone. Lester was a good guide and a hard worker. And he was very familiar with the area around Clearwater.

Barney remembered the first time he met Lester. It was when Lester's wife was asphyxiated. Barney drove them both to the hospital in the ambulance. Then he stayed with Lester while Doc Martin worked to save Millie's life. He and Lester got together again when Lester's son was getting into all kinds of trouble and Lester was trying to keep him out of jail.

When Barney got to town, he headed for the school. He drove around to the back, parked at the loading dock, and went into Lester's office. The light was on, but nobody was there, so Barney walked through the empty halls to the superintendent's office. When the secretary said she thought Lester was working in the chemistry lab, Barney went to find him. He tried the door, but it was locked. As he stood in the hall, trying to think of somewhere else to look, the door opened suddenly and Lester came out.

"Barney," said Lester who was quite surprised, "what are you doing here?"

"Hello, Lester." The two shook hands and Barney said, "I need your help."

"Help? What kind of help?"

"A young woman was killed last night over by Clearwater Lake, but we can't find her body. I need someone to help me do some tracking."

"Killed? How'd it happen?"

Barney went on to tell Lester what he knew about the killing. When he mentioned Dick, Lester interrupted.

"Are you talking about Dick Christopher?"

"Yes," said Barney. "Do you know him?"

"Sure I do. He and I went to high school together. He came by the house last Saturday and asked me where he ought to go canoeing. What's he doing over in that area?"

"He's camped on the south side of Gogebic. He ran into the dead woman's friend this morning and is going to stay with her tonight at his campsite. She doesn't want to come back until we find her friend."

"Do you want me to come out and try to help you find the dead woman's body?" asked Lester.

"Yes," said Barney, "I do. You've got a good dog, and you know the area. With your help we should be able to find her right away. I also need you to help me find a camera."

"A camera?" asked Lester.

Barney told Lester about the camera and how Lisa had used the flash to try to scare off a bear. "It probably flew out of her hand when she got shot," said Barney. "We still haven't found it. But if the film is still good, we might have a picture of the killer."

"Gee, I'm sorry, Barney, but I won't be able to help you in the morning. I've got too much work to do here. But if you still want me, I'll try to get away about noon."

"Well half a day is better than none," said Barney. "Call my office before you start out. Maggie will tell you where we are and how to get there. She can save you a trip out if we've already found what we're looking for."

Barney and Lester talked for a few minutes more, and then Barney went home to his wife and two little daughters. He wanted to take a hot shower and get into some dry clothes before he went back to his office to make out his reports.

After Barney left, Lester went back into the chemistry lab and locked the door.

Alex Craig was on the portage between East and West Pike when he received a radio message from Camp Menogyn. The camp director said it was all right for him to stop by the island in West Pike and drop off the canoe he'd found. Alex was bringing his group back to camp when the message came, so he decided to drop the canoe off as they headed down the lake.

"Eric, you and Tom come with me. We're going to get rid of the canoe we found. It belongs to two guys who're camping out on the island. I want the rest of you eight-balls to keep moving toward Clearwater. If you get to the west end before we catch up, stay at Nelson's Lodge. We'll get there as soon as we can."

"The way those guys paddle," said Eric, "we'll catch up with them before they reach the palisade."

His remark got an appropriate response from the other campers.

"Okay, you turkeys," said Alex. "Can the bullcrap and get moving. It's supposed to rain all night, and I don't want to be out here any longer than I have to. So come on, move it."

All three canoes started along the south shore of West Pike. When they had gone about a mile, they reached a dogleg in the lake. Alex sent two of the canoes across and down the north shore while he, Eric, and Tom stayed to the south and headed for the island. Bruno and Chet's canoe was being pulled behind at the end of a twenty-foot tether rope.

Alex scanned the island as they approached, but all he could see was a two-man tent that was pitched close to the south shore. He figured the two men were inside, trying to stay dry. He looked ahead and to his right and saw that the other two canoes were proceeding toward the Clearwater portage.

As Alex guided his canoe into the channel that separated the island from the south shore of the lake, he surveyed the campsite. It was a mess. Bottles and cans were littered everywhere. He knew right away that the two men were lousy campers. He also knew that by this time they should be pretty uncomfortable.

"Hold it here, Eric," said Alex when they were twenty feet from shore. He reached back and pulled the trailing canoe forward. A loud bang echoed across the water when the two aluminum canoes collided. Alex started to untie the tether rope when a head popped out of the tent.

"Hey," yelled Bruno, "is that our canoe?"

Chet's head also popped out. And in his eagerness to see what was happening, he knocked Bruno into a pool of water in front of their tent.

"You dumb son of a bitch," yelled Bruno.

Eric and Tom glanced back at Alex.

"I think this is your canoe," said Alex. "We found it beached at the east end of the lake." He gave the canoe a shove and sent it toward shore, but it stopped short of the beach and started to drift again.

"Go get the goddamn canoe," Bruno yelled to Chet. "Go on, go get it."

Chet crawled out of the tent in his barefeet with only his T-shirt and Levis on. He gingerly stepped across the wet ground and into the water. He grabbed the canoe and pulled it ashore.

"You'd better pull it way up, mister, or you'll lose it again," said Eric.

"We didn't lose it, kid," said Chet. "Some son of a bitch stole it from us."

Alex didn't like the looks of either one of these men. If Dick Christopher set their canoe adrift, he probably had a very good reason for doing so.

"Hey," yelled Bruno, "have you seen an older guy out here by himself, wearing a tan jacket and Levis?"

Alex hesitated to answer, but then said, "Yes, we saw him this morning over on the Clearwater-West Pike portage."

"That son of a bitch left us out here," said Chet. "We could've died."

Alex thought it might be fun to send these two on another wild-goose chase. He didn't think they'd leave the island as long as it was still raining. And if they got up to the Border Route Trail in the morning, there probably wouldn't be anybody there. "He's up on the Border Route Trail," he said.

"Where the hell is the Border Route Trail?" asked Bruno.

"It crosses the Clearwater-West Pike portage about three-fourths of the way toward Clearwater. You'll see a sign on your left where the Trail runs north and south. He's on the south side, right at the top of the hill. Just go up the Trail and you'll be sure to find him. It's right over there," said Alex as he pointed to the hills south and west of the island. Then he turned to his two young companions.

"Come on, Eric, let's get going. We've got some paddling to do to catch up with the rest of our group."

———

Neither Bruno nor Chet thanked the campers for bringing their canoe back. Chet had to climb over Bruno to get back into the tent and out of the rain. And before Bruno could get untangled from Chet, the campers were gone.

Bruno closed the tent flap and started putting on his boots. "We've got to get that son of a bitch," he said.

"Not in this rain, we're not," said Chet. "And besides, he's probably already gone from there."

The two argued then, but Chet prevailed. They were both cold, wet, and hungry, and the thought of paddling down the lake in the rain at the end of the day didn't seem like a very good idea to either one of them. They decided instead to spend one more night on the island. Then, rain or shine, they'd leave in the morning. If they found Dick, fine. Otherwise they'd both had enough of the north woods. They were going back to civilization. And if Cyrus Bransky wanted to keep hassling Dick Christopher, he'd just have to get somebody else to do it.

Bruno and Chet didn't know it at the time, but someone else was about to do more to frighten Dick Christopher than they had ever hoped to do.

It was still raining after the sun went down. Almost everyone in the BWCA was either in a tent or a cabin. And until the storm passed at midnight, no one was going to be outside if they didn't have to be.

Dick and Judy had spent a couple of hours in the clearing in the late afternoon, trying to find the camera and Lisa's body. Then, thoroughly soaked, they went back to Dick's campsite on Gogebic. Judy had taken her sleeping bag into Dick's tent and slept for a couple of hours. When she woke up, she found Dick, sitting under the tarpaulin, cooking stew for dinner. When it was ready, the two of them crowded into his tent to eat where it was dry.

As they ate, they talked about everything that had happened in the past twenty-four hours. Judy was still emotionally and physically exhausted, even after her long nap. So as soon as she finished eating, she got back into her sleeping bag and went to sleep.

Dick cleaned the cooking utensils and stowed them under his overturned canoe along with his and Judy's packs and Barney's two-way radio. He also checked his supply of dry birch bark and beaver wood that he had under the canoe. He thought about going back over to the clearing but decided against it because of the rain. Instead, he poured himself a capful of brandy, sat under the tarpaulin, and listened to the rain. Finally, at ten o'clock, he decided to get some sleep.

Judy was sound asleep when Dick crawled into his tent. In order to get out in the morning without disturbing her, he decided to sleep with his head toward the front flap.

Exhausted as Dick was, he was still unable to rest, let alone sleep. He lay in his sleeping bag for several minutes and thought about everything that was happening to him. He thought about Lisa's body lying out in the woods. And he thought about the killer and Judy and Ellen and the two men who were chasing him. His whole world seemed to be in turmoil. He'd come to the Gunflint Trail to get away from his troubles, but his troubles seemed to be growing and getting the best of him. He felt trapped, because he couldn't see a way out of it. His mind kept wandering from one thing to another.

It was warm inside the tent in spite of the overall cooling effect of the rain, so Dick unfastened the outer flap of the tent and loosely tied the mosquito netting on the inside. Then he lay back once more and tried to fall asleep. He finally dozed off about eleven o'clock.

At the west end of Clearwater, a dark van returned to the abandoned cabin site where it had been the night before. And again, a lone man launched his square-stern canoe into the water, started his electric outboard, and headed for the east end of the lake. Forty minutes later, he beached his canoe in the little cove beneath the palisade, pulled it ashore, and hid it in the woods. Then he started up the narrow path that led to the Border Route Trail above him.

The man stopped several yards short of the place where the two trails met. Then he turned and walked a few yards into the woods to a small mound of freshly cut cedar boughs. He removed the boughs and exposed the lifeless body of Lisa Murphy.

As he looked at the body, he thought about his reason for hiding her. He had hoped it would give him enough time to find her companion and look for the missing camera. But now, too many people had gotten involved. If he put the body back where it could be found, everybody might forget about the camera for a while. And if he could chase some of the people out of the area, he'd have more time by himself to look for it.

He lifted the body over his shoulder and continued up the trail. When he reached the Border Route Trail, he turned north to the point where it met a smaller trail that led through the aspen grove to the clearing where the woman had been killed. He laid the body down at the junction of the two trails, and then went through the woods to the clearing.

He took out his flashlight and shined it around the area. The two-man tent was still standing at the south edge of the clearing where he'd seen it the night before, so he went over and looked inside. Then he moved to the north edge of the clearing from where he'd fired his arrow. He retraced his steps across the clearing and looked for the young woman's camera. But the rain made it almost impossible to see anything past seven or eight feet from where he stood.

Frustrated by the rain and tall grass, the man decided to look for the dead woman's companion. He walked back to the south edge of the clearing and found another trail that headed east. He followed it until he came to a campsite on the south side of Gogebic. Then he turned off his flashlight, put it in his pocket, and cautiously approached the area.

The man saw a two-man tent that was pitched about six feet back from the edge of the lake. An overturned canoe was off to the left, and underneath it were two packs and some fishing gear. A tarpaulin was stretched out between two trees at a height of about six feet. The man listened, but all he could hear was the sound of the rain as it fell on the canoe, the tarp, the tent, and the forest around him.

The man stood looking at the tent for almost a minute and thought about the two people who were inside. When he was fully accustomed to the darkness, he moved toward the tent and saw that the front was facing the lake. Guylines at front and back were tied to two trees. The lines on the sides were tied to small stakes that had been tapped into the soft ground.

He untied the rear guyline and looped it around the tree. Then, as he walked forward, he played out the line so he could keep the tent upright. When he got to the other tree, he untied the front guyline.

There was barely enough rope to allow him to hold both guylines without letting the tent collapse. Then, with one quick move, he dropped the lines and grabbed the top of the tent. The stakes that held the sides of the tent pulled easily out of the wet ground as the man dragged the tent to the water's edge. By now, the two people in the tent were awake and thrown about as the tent was dragged toward the lake.

As soon as the man got the tent to the water, he moved quickly behind it and shoved as hard as he could. The tent and its occupants rolled over the edge of the shoreline and dropped into four feet of water.

The man stood and watched as the tent started to sink. Then, chuckling to himself, he turned and walked back along the trail he had just come over.

Dick woke up suddenly and felt his tent being dragged along the ground. He tried to get up, but Judy was lying on top of him and he was tangled up in his sleeping bag. Then he felt the ground drop away, and he knew they were in the water.

Enough air filled the tent to balloon it out above their heads, but Dick knew that water would soon rush in and displace the air. He and Judy had to get out of the tent right away or they'd drown.

Dick worked frantically at the mosquito netting and finally got it untied, even though Judy was still on top of him, trying to get out of her sleeping bag. She cried out several times as she tried to free herself, but there was little Dick could do to help her. He pulled the front of the tent over his head and held his breath. His head and shoulders were free, but his legs were still caught. He couldn't swim away from the tent, and he couldn't find anything to brace himself against to kick himself free.

Suddenly, the tent rolled over and started to move toward deeper water. That caused Judy to roll to one side and allowed Dick to get his legs out from under her. But his wet clothes, the tent, and his sleeping bag were all still holding him down. He thought his lungs were going to burst as he pulled the tent down over his waist. Then he finally got both legs free and shot to the surface. He filled his lungs with air and dove back for the tent and Judy.

Judy was still inside the tent, frantically trying to keep from drowning. Dick tried everything he could to get the tent on shore, but he was still six feet away. Everytime he tried to pull the tent, his feet would slip on the rocky lake bottom.

Just then the front guyline floated by. Dick grabbed it and pulled until he got ahold of the front peak of the tent. He pulled again, but the tent, which was now filling with water, was too heavy to move. He waded ashore with the guyline and tied it around a tree so the tent wouldn't slip into deep water. Then he pulled hard on the guyline and prayed that it wouldn't tear away from the top of the tent.

Dick was only three feet from shore now, but it seemed like a mile. He reached back with his left arm and wrapped it around a tree. Then he pulled as hard as he could with his right arm until he got the tent next to shore. He was still in four feet of water, so he dropped down and got under the tent. He pushed off the bottom and tried to lift the tent with Judy in it. At first, he just slid on the gravel bottom. But on the second try, he pushed as hard as he could and finally got Judy and the tent on shore. Then he got out of the water and tried to catch his breath.

Judy had been threshing around inside the tent when it was in the water, but now she was lying still. Dick hurried and untangled the tent and found the front flap. He pulled the tent up and over Judy's legs, which were still wrapped in her sleeping bag. Then he pulled Judy free of the tent and threw it aside.

He rolled Judy over on her stomach and pulled the wet sleeping bag away. Then he straddled her back and pushed hard against her ribs to force out any water she might have swallowed. She still didn't show signs of breathing, so he rolled her over on her back and started mouth-to-mouth resuscitation. Within seconds she was gasping for air and reaching out for him. He held her close as she started to cry.

Dick and Judy hung on to each other for several minutes, seeking comfort from the terrifying experience they'd just gone through. Then Dick helped Judy move under the tarpaulin and out of the rain. They were both soaking wet.

Dick went over to his canoe and got out his candle lantern. He lit it and hung it on the tree beneath the tarp. Then he turned to Judy.

"Are you okay?" he asked.

"I guess so," she said.

"Well somebody out there doesn't like us," said Dick as he looked around the campsite. Until then he hadn't even thought that the person who pushed them in the lake might still be close by, watching them from the darkness of the woods. But he was too exhausted to be frightened. He turned back to Judy.

"You'd better get some dry clothes on," he said. "Do you have some here?"

"Yes," said Judy, "they're in my pack, under the canoe."

Dick got a dry towel from under the canoe and gave it to Judy, but she just sat on the log and stared at it.

"Come on," said Dick, "I'll help."

He took the towel and dried her hands and face. Then he unbuttoned her wool shirt. She looked right at him with a surprised look on her face, but she didn't move to stop him. Dick took off her shirt and the T-shirt she wore underneath. Then he reached behind her and unhooked her bra. She let it slide down her arms as he pulled it toward him. Then he took the towel and dried her off.

Dick had undressed women before as a prelude to lovemaking, but this was obviously not the same thing. Judy was a very attractive woman, and drying her off aroused him sexually. But at the same time, he felt a closeness to her that went beyond his sexual desire.

As the cool night air began to revive her, she asked for her pack that was under her canoe. When Dick brought it to her, she opened it, got out a dry bra, and put it on. Then she got out a wool shirt and a Ragg knit sweater and put them on too.

"You'd better get some dry Levis on," said Dick. "Can you manage all right?"

"Yes, I'm all right now. Thank you." She got out a pair of pants, dry Levis, and socks. She also got out a pair of camp moccasins to replace her boots which were still in the tent.

"I'll empty out the tent," said Dick as he stepped out from under the tarpaulin. "It looks like it's finally stopped raining." He turned his back to Judy and pulled the wet sleeping bags out of the tent. There wasn't much privacy in the woods, but Dick tried to provide what he could.

As Judy changed clothes behind him, Dick got everything out of the tent, including his boots, Buck knife, and waterproof alarm clock. He also got out a lot of water. He had to shake the tent a couple of times before Judy's soggy boots fell on the ground. He hung the tent over a tree branch and laid the two sleeping bags over his clothesline.

"You'd better change now too," said Judy as she finished dressing.

Dick turned and saw Judy drying her hair with a towel.

"How are you doing?" he asked.

"I'm okay now," she said. "Someone tried to kill us, didn't they?"

"Yes," said Dick, "they sure as hell did."

"But who did it, and why?"

"I'm not sure, but it was probably the same person who killed Lisa. Either he thinks you can identify him, or we have a psycho running around loose. As soon as the sun comes up, I'll call the YMCA camp and have them contact the sheriff. This is getting out of hand."

"Do you think he's still out there?" asked Judy with an anxious look at the dark woods that surrounded them.

"I don't think so. If he was, he probably would have paid us another visit by now. And don't forget, it could be more than one person if those two Indians are involved."

"What time is it?" asked Judy.

"My trusty waterproof alarm clock says it's five after one. We still have five hours left before the sun comes up. I might as well build a fire now that the rain has stopped."

Dick got dry beaver wood and birch bark from under the canoe and built a nice, warm fire. He also got out his single-burner propane stove and some hot chocolate mix. Then, after he changed into dry clothes, he and Judy sat by the fire and waited for the dawn.

At the west end of Clearwater, the man who had dumped them in the lake lifted his square-stern canoe up on his cartop carrier, got in his van, and drove back to Grand Marais. The rain had stopped, and the moon was starting to shine through the broken clouds. It was turning out to be a lovely night.

✒︎THURSDAY

The sky was clear and the air was crisp and cool when the sun came up at six o'clock. Last night's rain had made everything smell fresh and clean again. It looked like it was going to be another beautiful day in the BWCA. Dick and Judy had been sitting in front of their fire since their unexpected plunge into the lake. When the sun came up, Dick added more beaver wood to the fire and started boiling water on his propane stove.

"How are you feeling now?" he asked Judy.

"Like I've been through the wringer a couple of times. I'm sore all over and completely exhausted."

"Let's get some breakfast." said Dick. "If you'll fix the hot chocolate, I'll go pick some berries. I think raspberry pancakes would taste good this morning. When I get back, I'll radio Camp Menogyn. They can call the sheriff and tell him what happened out here last night."

Dick gathered blueberries and raspberries as he walked along the trail that led to the west end of the lake. The berries were plentiful, and it didn't take him long to fill his cooking pot. He looked for footprints or other signs of the intruder who'd pushed them into the lake, but he couldn't find anything. When he got back to his campsite, Judy had a cup of hot chocolate waiting for him.

Dick gave the berries to Judy, got on the radio, and called the YMCA camp. Dick told the director what had happened and asked him to call the sheriff. Then Dick and Judy sat by the fire, ate breakfast, and waited for the sheriff to come back out.

Barney Ross got to his office at six-thirty. He arrived just in time to take a call from the camp director from Menogyn. When he found out that someone had tried to kill Dick and Judy the night before, he decided he'd better go back out right away.

Barney called his two deputies, Don Waters and Maynard Johnson, and told them he'd be by their homes in a few minutes to pick them up. Then he called the emergency room at the hospital and asked the staff to tell Doc Martin that he might have to come out and examine a body—if Barney could find it.

As he drove over to pick up his deputies, he saw that Lester's pickup truck was already at the high school. "He sure gets to school early," thought Barney. "I can't imagine why he'd be working so hard in the summer when the kids are out of school."

Don Waters was waiting for Barney when he drove up the driveway. He said hello and handed Barney a cup of hot coffee as he got into the Blazer.

"You're a good man, Don Waters," said Barney as he took a sip of coffee, backed out of the driveway, and went to get his other deputy. "Are you ready to do some hunting?"

"About as ready as I'll ever be," said Don.

"What did you find out about the helicopter?"

"The Forest Service says we can have it anytime we want it. All we have to do is let 'em know. They'll drop what they're doing and come right out. And they'll bring Doc Martin with them."

"How long are they going to have the helicopter up here?" asked Barney.

"They're using it for seeding and stocking all week. So if we don't find the woman's body today, we'll still be able to have it for the next couple of days."

"What about Doc? Will he be around?"

"No problem," said Don. "He's going to keep his schedule open so he can come out whenever we need him."

"Things are getting wild out there, Don. We almost had another killing last night."

"Another one? Who? Where?"

"Same place," said Barney. "The murdered woman's friend and the man who found her. They were in his tent around midnight when somebody dumped them into Gogebic Lake. I guess they had a helluva time getting out alive."

"What's going on out there?" asked Don.

"I don't know," said Barney. "But I hope we find that woman's body and get some answers today. I want to get this thing settled."

"At least we're going to have a break in the weather," said Don. "The forecast calls for several days of sunshine. We shouldn't get anymore rain until after the weekend."

"If that's the case," said Barney, "we might find her before noon. Then we're going to have to bring in Red Hawk and his uncle."

"Do you still think they're mixed up in this?"

"It sure looks like it. But whether they are or not, we're going to have to bring them in, because they were in the area when the woman was killed."

After Barney picked up his other deputy, the three of them headed up the Gunflint Trail for Clearwater Lake.

Bruno and Chet had been having a hard time getting up in the morning since they came up north. But when they woke up this morning, they were alert and ready for action. They had their canoe back, and they thought they knew where Dick Christopher was.

They ate a cold breakfast, packed up all their gear, and loaded their canoe. At seven-thirty they pushed off the island and headed toward the Clearwater-West Pike portage. Twenty-five minutes later, they unloaded their canoe at the west end of the lake. Chet took the packs and canoe paddles, and Bruno took the canoe. They had walked for ten minutes on the portage when Chet spotted the Border Route Trail sign.

"Here it is," he said to Bruno.

"Okay, let's dump the stuff here."

"Where?" asked Chet. "There isn't any room unless you want to toss it in the woods."

"Then toss it in the woods," said Bruno. "Nobody is going to bother it anyway. Just get it back far enough so it won't be seen."

The two of them moved back about ten yards into the woods and set their canoe and camping equipment on the ground. Then they hurried back to the Border Route Trail and started up the hill.

If Bruno and Chet had stayed on the portage all the way to the Clearwater landing, they'd have run into Barney Ross. He and his two deputies had just arrived at the landing and were pulling their boat ashore.

Bruno and Chet had to slow down as they hiked up the hill. They came to an abrupt stop when Chet nearly stepped on Lisa's body. It was lying right in the middle of the Trail where it had been placed the night before.

"God almighty!" exclaimed Chet. "Look at this."

Bruno was following close behind and almost fell over Chet when he stopped.

"You dumb . . . Goddamn! Is she dead?"

"She sure looks dead. Jeeze, look at her chest. She must have been shot. Look at all the blood."

"She looks awful stiff," said Bruno. "Like she's been here a while."

"Do you think Christopher is mixed up in this?" asked Chet.

"How the hell would I know."

"So what are we going to do?"

"I think we ought to get the hell out of here," said Bruno. "I don't want to get mixed up in any of this."

"Are we just going to leave her here?"

"I'm not going to touch her," said Bruno. "Let somebody else find her. We'd just better get the hell out of here right now. Come on, let's go."

"You two aren't going anywhere. Just stand right where you are and don't move."

Bruno and Chet turned around and saw Barney Ross standing in the Trail, pointing a gun at them. Two other men were coming up the Trail behind him.

"Hey, we didn't do this," said Bruno.

"Yeah," said Chet. "We just found her here."

"Is that right?" asked Barney. "What are you men doing here anyway? You aren't hikers because you don't have any packs."

"We just came up here to look for somebody," said Bruno.

"Well it looks like you found her," said Barney. "You know, I've been looking all over the place for this young woman's body. Now you two show up and here she is, right in the middle of the Trail. How come?"

"Hey, we didn't do nothing," said Bruno. "We just found her. That's all."

"We'll have to see about that," said Barney. "Now turn around and put your hands on your heads. Don, Maynard, put cuffs on these two."

Bruno and Chet offered no resistance as they were being handcuffed. They knew they were in a bad situation, and they didn't want to do anything to make it worse. Besides, Barney still had his gun pointed at them.

"Maynard," said Barney, "go back to the boat and get the body bag. Then get on the radio and put in a call for Doc Martin. He'll have to come out before we can move her. And see if we can get him here in the helicopter. Otherwise we'll have to take her out in the boat." Then Barney turned to his other deputy.

"Don, let's take these two up to the clearing where this woman was killed. Then maybe they can tell us what's going on."

"We don't know nothing," said Bruno. "So help me God, we don't know nothing about this."

"Yeah," said Chet, "we don't know nothing."

"I can almost believe that," said Barney as he motioned for them to start walking.

The clearing looked no different to Barney than it did when he left it a day earlier. Dick and Judy were not there, so he thought they must still be over at the campsite on Gogebic.

"Don," said Barney, "I'm going over to get the people who are on Gogebic. You stay here and keep an eye on these two." Then he turned to Bruno and Chet and said, "You men sit on this log and don't try anything dumb. I don't want to have to take three bodies out of here today."

Barney left Bruno and Chet with his deputy and walked over to Dick's campsite.

Dick and Judy stood up nervously when they heard someone coming down the trail toward them. They were both relieved to see it was Barney.

"Good morning, sheriff," said Dick as he extended his hand. "It's good to see you again."

"Good morning," said Barney. "I understand you two had some trouble out here last night." He glanced around at all the gear that had been hung out to dry and asked what happened.

"Somebody tried to kill us," said Judy. "They dumped the tent into the lake while we were in it."

Barney listened as Dick and Judy described the nightmarish experience they'd gone through.

"It doesn't make sense," said Barney. "Something is awful screwed up here."

"Why do you say that?" asked Dick.

"If whoever did this really wanted you dead, they would've done a much better job of it. Sure, you could've drowned, but you were able to get out. It looks like the person who did it just tossed you in and took off. They must have wanted to scare you, not kill you. Otherwise they'd have banged you on the head while you were trying to get to shore."

"Well if they were trying to scare us, they sure did a good job of it."

"And they almost killed us," added Judy.

"We can go over the details later," said Barney. "Something else has happened." He turned to Judy and said, "We found Lisa's body."

Judy stiffened and tears came to her eyes.

"As a matter of fact," said Barney, "*we* didn't find her. Two other guys did. I think they're the two goons you were talking about, Dick."

"Where is she?" asked Judy.

"She's over on the Border Route Trail. I don't want to move her until the County Coroner can examine her."

"Can I go to her now?" asked Judy.

"Yes, I wish you would," said Barney, "because we'll need a proper identification. It won't be pretty, but I guess you already know that."

"What about the men who found her?" asked Dick. "Where are they?"

"We've got them trussed up over in the clearing. Why don't we all go over there now?"

—

When Dick, Judy, and Barney walked into the clearing, Don Waters was still standing behind Bruno and Chet.

"Well hello, gentlemen," said Dick. "What brings you two up here?"

"You son of a bitch," said Bruno.

"Hey, that's no way to talk," said Barney. "Do you know these two men, Dick?"

"Yes, in a way. I think they were hired to harass me by a man I work with back in Minneapolis. My neighbor got roughed up when they forced their way into my condominium. They were going to do the same thing to me over on West Pike until I took their canoe away from them."

"Do you think they're the ones who tried to kill you last night?" asked Barney.

"Could be," said Dick.

"Hey, wait a minute," said Bruno. "We didn't do nothing last night. We were stranded out on that goddamn island."

"Did anyone see you out there?" asked Barney.

"Yeah, the kids who brought our canoe back," said Bruno.

"And did they stay with you all night?"

"No, they left right away."

"So nobody saw you last night."

"Well, no," admitted Bruno.

"Then I'm probably going to have to consider you two as suspects," said Barney.

"What for?" asked Chet.

"Attempted murder."

"Hey, wait a minute," said Bruno.

"You can't do that," said Chet.

"Oh yes I can," said Barney. "You guys forget. I'm the sheriff. I arrest people who break the law. It's my job."

"But we didn't do nothing," pleaded Chet.

"We'll decide that after we talk a while."

Then Judy stepped up to Barney. "Can I see Lisa now?" she

asked.

"Yes, of course. Don, you stay here while I take Judy down to the Trail. Dick, you'd better come too."

Maynard had covered Lisa's body with the canvas bag. When the three of them got there, he uncovered her face so Judy could identify her.

"That's Lisa," said Judy as she tried to choke back her tears.

Dick held her then and let her cry on his shoulder. Judy had been through a harrowing experience and now she was finally letting all her emotions come out.

"Maynard, did you get in touch with the hospital?" asked Barney.

"Yes," said Maynard, "and I also asked the Forest Service if they'd bring their helicopter out. They were over on Devil's Track Lake when I called, but they should be able to pick up Doc and get out here in a half hour."

Barney went over and put his arm on Judy's shoulder.

"When Doc gets through here, I'd like you to go back with him. My secretary will be waiting for you at the Court House. We'll have to get a statement from you and make arrangements for Lisa's body. And if you're up to it, I'd like you to call Lisa's parents for us." Then he turned to Dick.

"Dick, I'd like you to help us bring back all the camping gear that belongs to Judy and Lisa. And before everybody gets out of here, I'd like to search through the area around the clearing and see if we can't come up with Lisa's camera. Can you help us?"

"I'd be happy to," said Dick.

"Okay," said Barney, "let's go back to the clearing."

When the three of them returned to the clearing, Barney asked Judy to reconstruct the events of Tuesday night. She had a hard time remembering exactly where Lisa had been standing when she was hit with the arrow, because it had been dark then and now she was emotionally exhausted.

Don, Barney, and Dick fanned out over the entire area and looked for the camera and any other clues that might help them identify the killer. The only thing they were sure of was that the killer had been at the north edge of the clearing, probably at the head of the trail that went along the edge of the pond over to Gogebic. They were certain that Lisa had been shot somewhere between the north edge of the clearing and the tent.

"I think I can see what happened," said Barney as he stood in the middle of the clearing. "Lisa was hit somewhere in this area. Then the killer must have carried or dragged her body into the woods where we couldn't find it."

"I still can't understand why he hid her body," said Dick.

"I can't either," said Barney, "unless he just wanted to throw us off. I'd really like to get a dog out here and do some tracking. Then we'd at least know *where* her body was hidden. And speaking of tracking, Dick, I saw Lester Malone yesterday. He said the two of you went to high school together."

"Yes, we did," said Dick.

"Well I stopped by to see if he could help us here, but he couldn't come out this morning. He knows this area very well, and he has a good tracking dog. He said he could come out after noon if we didn't find Lisa's body before that. Now I'll have to call him and tell him not to come."

"I can't figure out how Lisa's body ended up back on the Border Route Trail," said Dick. "We went over that spot several times earlier, and it wasn't anywhere near there."

"Whoever killed Lisa and hid her body wanted it found again," said Barney. "It's probably the same person who paid you a visit last night. I'm not real good at figuring out why people do things like this, but I would guess he was poaching and panicked when Lisa and Judy came out of their tent. His shot was probably a reflex action rather than a deliberate attempt to kill. In either case, the results are the same.

"His first response was to hide the body. Then last night he had second thoughts about what he did, so he came back and put Lisa's body right out in the open where it would be found. He could've left you two alone, but he had some reason for trying to scare you. He probably just wanted to chase you out of here."

"It sure would help if we could find the camera," said Dick. "We might be able to see who the killer is."

"I think you're right about the camera," said Barney. "We should try to find it. But even if we don't, I'd bet money that Red Hawk and his uncle are the ones we're looking for. It had to be someone who knows this area, and that certainly fits those two. Besides. they're both pretty good with a bow and arrow, and on top of that, you apparently saw them coming and going through here Tuesday night. We'll bring them in as soon as we can, but we should still try to find that camera."

A half an hour later, the helicopter came in over the trees above the palisade. It hovered over the clearing for a few seconds while the pilot looked for a place to land. The helicopter had floats, so Barney motioned for the pilot to land on the pond. The pilot nodded and brought it down at the edge of the water. The downdraft scattered twigs and branches, rippled the water, and stirred up the long prarie grass that covered the clearing.

When the motor stopped, Barney helped Doc Martin step ashore. He told Doc where Lisa's body was and directed Don Waters to take him there. Then he turned to Judy.

"Judy," he said, "you'd better get your things together. You don't have to take all of it, just what you need now. Dick will bring the rest later today. I'd like you to go back in the helicopter with Doc as soon as he's ready."

Judy spent a few minutes in the tent putting things in her day pack. Then she went over to Dick.

"Thanks for all your help," she said. "And thanks for saving my life last night."

"I'm sorry your camping trip had to turn out this way," said Dick. "And from what Barney said, you've still got some unpleasant things to do when you get back to town. I'll bring the rest of your things when I come out this afternoon. If you're feeling up to it, I'd like to take you to dinner tonight."

"I'd like that," said Judy. She reached up and gave Dick a kiss on the cheek. Then she went over and climbed into the helicopter.

Maynard and Doc Martin came into the clearing then, carrying Lisa's body in the body bag. Dick and Barney helped load it in the helicopter. Then Doc climbed in next to Judy and they took off.

After the helicopter had gone, Dick, Barney, and the two deputies tried for an hour to find the camera.

"The only thing I can figure," said Barney, "is that somebody already has the camera or else it's in the pond. We sure as hell can't find it."

"It's like losing a golf ball," said Dick. "Someone else could walk in here and see it just like that. What do you want to do now?"

"We'll take these two back to town," said Barney as he motioned to Bruno and Chet. "I really don't think they're involved here at all. They just walked into the wrong place at the wrong time. But I'll do my best to put a scare into them before I send them back to Minneapolis. I'll tell them they're on probation, and if they do anything to you, we'll drag them back up here and slap them in jail."

"I'd appreciate that," said Dick. "I don't want those two clowns following me around everywhere I go."

"Then I'd like you to pack up all this gear and bring it back with you," said Barney. "We're going to have our hands full taking these two back with their canoe and all their gear."

"It might take a while," said Dick. "But I should be able to get all this stuff back to Grand Marais by late afternoon."

They said goodbye then, and Barney and his deputies took Chet and Bruno down to Clearwater and on to Grand Marais. Dick was left alone, or so he thought.

———

After everyone had gone, Dick went back to Gogebic and packed up all his gear. Most of it was still wet, but he thought he could dry it out when he got to Grand Marais. Either that or he'd take it back to Minneapolis and dry it there.

Dick also had to get his canoe over to Clearwater. He thought it would be too hard to carry it over to the clearing and down the Border Route Trail, so he paddled across Gogebic and took it down to West Pike. He found it was a lot easier going down than coming up.

When he got to West Pike, he paddled directly to the Clearwater portage. Then he picked up his canoe and carried it over the half-mile portage to the Clearwater landing. When he got there, he tipped his canoe over on its side and left it at the edge of the woods.

Without wasting any time, Dick hiked back up the Border Route Trail, went through the clearing, and returned to Gogebic. He closed down his campsite and took his gear back to where he'd left Lisa and Judy's things. He realized then that the area had really been stirred up when the helicopter landed and took off. The clearing looked quite a bit different than it did when he and Judy first walked over it. The grass around the pond had been blown flat against the ground and leaves were scattered everywhere. He thought he'd try one more time to find Lisa's camera, but only after he took all the camping gear down to the Clearwater landing.

Dick made two trips to Clearwater and stowed the gear under his overturned canoe. When he finished, he headed back to the clearing for the last time. He was getting tired from hiking up and down the steep trail, and he needed a rest. So he stopped at the top of the hill just before he got to the trail that led to the clearing.

As he looked around, he found another trail that headed west and continued toward the top of the palisade that rose above the south shore of Clearwater Lake. He followed the trail with his eyes until it disappeared into the trees. He wondered if it went all the way to the palisade or even to the west end of Clearwater. Then, when he felt rested, he turned and headed toward the clearing.

He had only walked a short distance along the trail in the aspen grove when he saw something that made him stop. Leaning against a tree about twenty feet from the side of the trail was a bow and a quiver of arrows. He knew they weren't there when he made his last trip down to the landing, so whoever left them had to be in the clearing ahead of him. He left the bow and arrows where he found them and cautiously approached the clearing. He stopped again when he saw Lester Malone.

Lester was walking very slowly along the edge of the pond as though he were looking for something. Dick thought then that the bow and quiver of arrows must belong to Lester, but he wondered why Lester had left them in the woods. And what, he wondered, was Lester looking for?

Dick started toward the clearing, but then he hesitated. Lester had dropped down on one knee at the edge of the pond and was reaching into the tall grass. When he stood up, he had Lisa's camera in his hand. It looked to Dick as if Lester was trying to get the back off the camera. Dick walked into the clearing then and called out to his old high school classmate.

"Hello, Lester."

Lester swung around to face Dick and almost dropped the camera.

"Dick, where'd you come from? I thought everybody had gone."

"I'm the only one left," said Dick. "But what are you doing here. And what did you find there?"

"Barney said you might need some help, so I came out when I could. I just found this camera. I guess it belongs to the girl who got killed."

"You're right," said Dick, who was still surprised at Lester's presence. "We've been trying to find that camera all day. Why don't you give it to me?"

"No, that's okay," said Lester as he held the camera close to his body. "I'll take it in to Barney. You've probably got a lot of other stuff to take back with you."

Dick was surprised at Lester's reaction. He wondered if Lester had been back in the woods waiting until everyone had gone. For some reason, things just didn't look right to Dick.

"Is that your bow and quiver of arrows back on the trail?"

"Ah . . . yes, it is," said Lester. "Why?"

"How come you left them back there?"

"I didn't think it would look very good if I came in here with a bow and arrow. Especially after what happened to that girl."

"How'd you get in here? You didn't come up from Clearwater because I'd have seen you on the Border Route Trail."

"You're sure asking a lot of questions," said Lester.

"I'm just trying to figure things out," said Dick. "Have you been up here before?"

It was obvious to Dick that his questions were making Lester very nervous. That prompted him to ask more questions.

"You didn't happen to come by here last night, did you?" asked Dick. "Or maybe the night before?"

Lester didn't answer. He just stood there, looking at the camera in his hand. Then he looked at the pond, the trees, the far side of the clearing—everywhere but at Dick.

"What's going on, Lester? What happened here?"

"Nothing," said Lester. "I just came out here to look for this camera."

"I think there's more to it than that," said Dick. As he watched Lester he quickly put things together in his mind. To start with, Lester had tried to discourage him from coming to this part of the BWCA. And Lester knew this area as well as anyone, including the two Indians. Besides that, Lester was a good hunter, especially with a bow and arrow. To Dick, it looked like Lester could be a prime suspect in Lisa's killing. He decided to go for a long shot.

"Is that your picture in the camera, Lester?"

"Could be."

"Could be? Is that all you have to say? Goddamnit, Lester, did you kill that girl?"

"What do you think?"

"I hate to say it, but I think you might have done it."

Lester looked at the camera in his hand and shook his head. "Oh boy," he said with a shrug of his shoulders. "I sure didn't want it to turn out like this." Then he turned and threw the camera into the middle of the pond.

"What the hell did you do that for," demanded Dick.

"I think you already know why," said Lester.

"Damnit, Lester. Why? Why did you do it?"

"Because that dumb little girl scared me half to death," said Lester who was now showing signs of anger. "I didn't know who or what was out there. And when that flash went off, so did I. She shouldn't have done that."

"But what were you doing here? And at that time of night?"

"I was picking up some merchandise," said Lester as he looked back at the pond.

"Merchandise?" asked Dick.

"Yeah," said Lester without looking at Dick. "I'm in the import business. Two friends of mine from Canada left a couple of bundles for me to pick up. We've done that quite a few times. I take the goods to town, process the contents at the school, and collect the money from a guy in Duluth who picks it up when it's ready."

"What are you dealing with? Drugs? Contraband?"

"A little bit of everything. Hashish, cocaine. Just about anything these guys think will sell."

"God almighty, Lester, you're crazy."

"Am I?" shouted Lester as he turned to face Dick. "You know about Millie. Do you have any idea what it cost me to take care of her? Do you know how much I make in a year at the school and working as a guide? I need the money, Dick, lots of it. And this is the best way I know for getting as much as I need in a hurry. All I have to do is move the stuff. I don't sell it. I don't use it. I just get paid for moving it from one place to another. It's that simple."

"It's not simple anymore, Lester. You killed somebody while you were doing it."

"It was an accident," said Lester. "I'm sorry it happened, but it was her fault. You don't go running around the north woods shooting off flash bulbs at people."

"You don't go around killing people either, Lester. Did you try to kill me last night?"

"Hell no, I didn't try to kill you. I just wanted to scare you so you'd get out of here where you don't belong. You should never have come up here in the first place."

"Well you shouldn't have killed Lisa either, Lester. You're in real big trouble."

"No I'm not," said Lester. "You are." He took a Buck knife out of his jacket pocket, opened it, and started toward Dick.

"For God's sake, Lester, don't do something stupid."

"I already have, Dick, and you're the only one who knows about it. I'm sorry, but I can't let you stay around to tell everybody else what I've done. There's too much at stake for me to let you go on living."

The two of them were not evenly matched. Even though Dick was much quicker, Lester was bigger and stronger. Dick knew he had to run to get away from Lester, but he didn't know where to go. When Lester lunged at him, Dick jumped aside and moved toward the woods.

When Lester lunged at him again, Dick fell down as he tried to step aside. He rolled over, got to his knees, and picked up a rock about the size of an orange. He threw it as hard as he could and hit Lester square in the chest.

Lester doubled over and gasped for air. In an instant, Dick picked up a tree limb and busted it against the side of Lester's head. The blow opened a deep gash in Lester's cheek and forehead. Blood gushed from the wound and flowed down Lester's face and neck.

Dick picked up another club and swung again at Lester's head. This time he hit Lester on the shoulder and dropped him to his knees. Then Dick threw the club at Lester and ran toward the Border Route Trail.

When Dick got through the aspen grove, he turned and started toward the Clearwater landing. But then he stopped and tried to figure out what kind of boat Lester had. If it was a canoe, Dick might be able to outrun him. But if Lester had a motorboat, Dick knew he'd be in trouble.

Dick decided he'd have a much better chance if he ran through the woods. He might even make it to the west end of Clearwater before Lester caught him. So he turned on the deer trail he had seen earlier and headed west toward the palisade. He hoped he'd be able to find his way to Nelson's Lodge, seven miles through the woods.

Dick turned and looked back to see if Lester was coming. When he did, he tripped over a tree root and fell. He twisted his wrist under him and cracked his bad knee on a rock. He got up right away and started to run again, but his knee collapsed under him. He got up again and forced himself to run, because he knew Lester would be after him in a minute.

Back in the clearing, Lester got to his feet with blood still running down the side of his head. He was groggy from Dick's blow, but he managed to get across the clearing to the aspen grove. He picked up his bow and quiver of arrows and staggered to the Border Route Trail. Then he stopped and listened. He could hear Dick running in the woods ahead of him toward the palisade. He strung an arrow and went after him.

Dick was having a hard time following the trail he'd chosen. It was steeper now and harder to climb, and his knee was starting to throb. He paused to rest and wished he hadn't. An arrow glanced off a tree to his right and burrowed into a pile of leaves. Dick couldn't see Lester, but he knew he was right behind him. He turned and started running up the trail again.

Lester was an excellent tracker and Dick's trail was easy to follow. The gap between them was narrowing rapidly. Lester's shoulder was causing a lot of pain, but if he braced himself against a tree, he could still shoot an arrow with accuracy. He was bleeding a lot, however, and that bothered him when he tried to aim.

Dick came to a clearing and sprinted across it. He felt it was useless to look back to see if Lester was coming; he knew he was. When he got across the clearing, he lost the trail and started to panic. Then, without looking to see where he was going, he charged ahead into the woods.

As he fought his way through the brush and branches, Dick saw another clearing to his right and ran toward it. The forest closed quickly around him again, and then suddenly, he faced nothing but open sky. He had reached the top of the palisade above Clearwater.

There were no trees along the edge, just scrub spruce and blueberry bushes. He ran on, jumping from rock to rock. Then he fell again and landed on his good knee. He had instinctively put out his wrist to break his fall, and he thought he heard a bone snap when he went down.

The pain of his injuries caused a wave of nausea to sweep over him. He tried to get up, but his knee gave out on him and he fell back to the rocky ledge. The pain in his knee shot down to his ankle and up to his hip. His leg started to feel numb, like it was asleep. He looked for cover, but there wasn't any. Then he saw Lester.

Lester was standing above Dick, next to a tree about thirty yards away. An arrow was already strung in the bow he held in his left hand.

Dick looked behind him at the lake that stretched out from the palisade. It was almost a 250-foot drop to the glacial deposits of boulders that fanned out into the lake.

Then Dick saw a boat. Two fishermen who were trolling across the front edge of the boulder field had cut their motor and were moving with the current. Dick crawled close to the edge and yelled down to them as loud as he could.

"Help! Help! Hey, up here! Help!"

The fishermen looked up, but they couldn't see anything on the cliff except the scrub pine that was silhouetted against the sky. Dick yelled again. Then he tried to stand so they could see him. But it was no use. He couldn't get up.

Dick looked back at Lester who was still standing above him, out of sight of the fishermen below. Then he turned and yelled again. But this time the fishermen didn't even look up. Instead, they started up their motor, swung around, and headed back up the lake to resume their drift across the front of the palisade.

Dick's heart sank when he heard the motor. He screamed again as loud as he could, but he knew it was futile. He turned again and looked up at Lester.

"I don't need this," said Lester as he put down his bow and arrow and started walking toward Dick. "I'll just help you over the edge. Then people will think you fell on your own."

Dick looked frantically around him for a weapon as Lester came toward him. His hand closed on a rock. When Lester reached down to grab him, Dick lunged forward and swung the rock against Lester's skull. The blow opened another gash above Lester's eye. Stunned, he fell backward against the rocks. Then he staggered to his feet with more blood running down his face.

"You son of a bitch!" he yelled at Dick. "You really piss me off."

Lester stepped back and picked up a large tree branch. He wedged it between two rocks and broke it in two. Then he picked up a piece that was about five feet long and as big around as a baseball bat.

"I'm going to bash your goddamn head in."

Lester came at Dick again with the club above his head. His face was contorted with hate and covered with blood.

Then suddenly, Lester's expression changed to one of frightened surprise. His large body seemed to float above Dick as he plummeted over the edge of the cliff with an arrow protruding from his chest. There was no scream, only the sound of the wind whispering through the trees. Lester was probably dead before he began his dive to the rocks below.

Dick wheeled around to see the Indian called Hawk standing above him, holding Lester's bow in his hand. Then everything went blank as Dick lost consciousness.

FRIDAY

Dick woke up in the Grand Marais hospital. When he was brought back to town the night before, Doc Martin thought it would be a good idea to keep him overnight for observation. Dick had several bumps and bruises, a badly sprained wrist, and a fairly serious contusion on his right knee. He was lying in bed, thinking about everything that had happened to him in the past few days when a nurse came in the room.

"Good morning," she said. "Do you feel like having breakfast?"

"That would be great," said Dick. "I didn't get any dinner last night, and I'm really starved."

"I'll bring a tray right away," said the nurse. "Then I'll call the sheriff. He wanted us to get in touch with him as soon as you were awake."

When the nurse left, Dick showered, shaved, and got dressed in clean clothes. The nurse brought in his tray just as he finished dressing.

"The sheriff will be here in about twenty minutes," she said. "That will give you plenty of time to eat."

Dick ate everything that was on his tray. He was famished, and the food was remarkably good. He was finishing his coffee when Barney came into his room with Judy and Hawk. Dick shook hands with Barney and Hawk and exchanged hugs with Judy. Then he turned to Hawk.

"A special good morning to you, Hawk. Thanks again for saving my life."

"How are you feeling?" asked the Indian.

"Sore all over, but rested. This place is more like a hotel than a hospital. I'm really glad to see all of you. But is this a social call or are you

137

here on business?"

"A little of both," said Barney. "I'd like you to give us a statement before you head back to Minneapolis."

"And I'd like to ask a favor," said Judy. "Can I ride with you as far as Duluth? I'm going to fly back to Chicago this afternoon."

"That's no problem," said Dick. "I'd be happy to do it. Barney, what's going to happen to Lester's family?"

"They're pretty stunned right now, but I think they'll be all right. Lester had a good insurance policy with the school, so they won't be hurting financially. And their daughter Ruth will be able to keep things going after the insurance money is gone. His son thinks he knows who Lester was working with and wants to help us put 'em away. So we've got some good leads to work with. Or I should say Hawk does."

"Hawk?" asked Dick.

"You tell him, Hawk," said Barney as he turned to the Indian.

"I didn't tell you last night when we brought you in, because there was too much going on. I'm a special agent for the U.S. Treasury Department. I've been working up here for almost three years, trying to stop the flow of drugs and contraband that goes back and forth across the Canadian border."

"Is that what Lester was involved in?" asked Dick.

"Yes," said Hawk. "He got sucked into it by some big spenders from Chicago. He was guiding them on a fishing trip when the subject of drug use came up. He told them about the drug traffic he'd seen in the schools along the north shore, in the resorts, in the ski areas, and in the colleges around Duluth.

"Those guys checked it out and saw the potential for some real good money to be made. Lester was vulnerable because of his wife's medical bills. He was working long hours at the school and hiring out as a guide to try to make ends meet. They made him an offer for some good money and he took it."

"How big an operation was it?" asked Dick.

"Not very big by Chicago standards," said Hawk. "But those guys got all the action, because no one else was moving it in or out of the area. They were able to come up here three or four times a year to do some fishing, snowmobiling, or skiing and take care of business at the same time. It was a vacation for them; it was salvation for Lester."

"How did you get involved?"

"The Treasury Department knew the stuff was trickling in, and they wanted it stopped. Lots of kids come up here every year, and they didn't want a major problem to get started in the area. They went to the State Attorney General down in St. Paul and asked for suggestions. When they started talking about an undercover agent, he suggested me. I'd worked as an intern in his office while I was going to law school. He knew what had happened to my folks, so he flew up here and asked if I'd help him. He offered me a fresh start and I was happy to take it. It got me and my uncle working again, and it allowed me to start taking law-school courses by correspondence."

"Did Barney know you were involved?" asked Dick.

"No, nobody did, except the Attorney General and the people in Washington."

"Did you know Lester was involved with the men from Chicago?"

"No," said Hawk, "but last week we traced a shipment to his pickup spot. If Lisa and Judy had not camped where they did, we would've run into him Tuesday night. When we saw the women there, we backed away, thinking we'd been given wrong information. If we'd have stayed, we'd have run into Lester for sure."

"I saw you come across Gogebic. Did you know I was there?"

"Not until we came back. But you didn't look like the kind of person we were looking for, so we didn't stop. That's such a remote little lake that very few people go up there. We came in that way because we were told the stuff was being brought in from Canada through Gogebic. And besides, we didn't want to stumble on someone coming up the Border Route Trail."

"What were you doing with the bow and quiver of arrows?"

"Almost everyone, including Barney here, thinks my uncle and I are into poaching. If we ever run into somebody while we're working on Treasury business, we'd rather have them think we were poaching. Then too, it's nice to have something along that we can protect ourselves with if we have to."

"Why did Lester pick that area?"

"Three reasons mostly. Clearwater Lake is on the edge of the BWCA, so he could use a motorboat if he had to. And it's very close to the Canadian border. But most important, it was a remote and isolated area that he and his partners had ready access to. And he knew where he was going when he got there."

"Well," said Dick, "I'm glad you arrived when you did. But how did you happen to be there yesterday?"

"My uncle and I heard what happened to Lisa, and we knew Barney was looking for us. I tried to get to the clearing before everyone had gone so we could clear ourselves. But just as I came up the Border Route Trail, I saw Lester heading into the woods with his bow and arrow. His face was all bloody and I knew he was mixed up in something.

"I went to the clearing and saw the camping gear, but I didn't see anyone else around. Then I figured Lester was probably chasing someone. I took out after him, but I had a hard time following him. When I reached the top of the palisade and saw what he was going to do to you, I had to act quickly. I hated to kill him, but I couldn't think of anything else to do. He was acting crazy, and I thought he'd have you over the edge before I could stop him."

"I really appreciate what you did for me," said Dick, "but I feel bad about the way it ended. If Lester hadn't found the camera, we might never have known that he was involved."

"What happened to the camera?" asked Barney.

"Lester tossed it into the middle of the pond," said Dick. "I suppose you can still get it out if you want the pictures."

"No thanks," said Judy. "I don't want anything around that's going to remind me of the terrible time we had there."

"If you're ready," said Barney, "we'd better get on over to the Court House. We still have some things to take care of."

After Dick said goodbye to Hawk, he rode over to the Court House with Barney and Judy. He talked into Barney's tape recorder for thirty minutes, telling everything he could remember about the whole bizarre episode at the clearing. When he finished, he and Judy walked out to the parking lot with Barney. Dick's station wagon had been brought down from Nelson's and was all packed and ready to go.

"Will you folks be coming back soon?" asked Barney.

"I won't," said Judy. "I love this area, but I spent most of my time up here with Lisa. If I came back, I'd think about her and everything that happened this week. I don't think I'll ever get over that. So I think it's time to find another place and another friend."

"I'll be back," said Dick. "I feel too close to this area not to come back. Only next time I'll come under different conditions, and I'll meet it with different expectations. But yes, I'll be back."

"Well when you do," said Barney, "be sure to come and see me. Goodbye, and good luck to both of you."

Dick and Judy both shook hands with Barney. Then they got into Dick's station wagon and headed down U.S. 61 to Duluth. Their adventure in the BWCA was over. Judy was going home to peace and quiet and temporary sadness. But Dick was headed for another maelstrom with Cyrus Bransky.

⏤

Cyrus called his secretary and told her he'd be coming in late for work. He had a two o'clock meeting with Timothy Abernathy, but he wanted to meet with Bruno first to find out what had happened to Christopher.

Cyrus and Bruno met again at the Rainbow Cafe. Cyrus listened as Bruno described everything that happened to him and Chet in the four days they were gone. The more Bruno talked, the more Cyrus felt as though he should never have sent those two idiots to harass Christopher. He thought he could almost have done better himself. He was pleased, however, when Bruno told him that Christopher had almost been killed twice.

Cyrus was very disappointed that Bruno and Chet had not had a chance to confront Christopher directly. Christopher may have had some harrowing experiences, but nothing seemed to happen to make him want to leave the company. Cyrus didn't know if Christopher even thought about his job while he was up north. It looked very much as if Bruno and Chet's trip was a big waste of time and money.

Cyrus seemed to be doing better on his own. He'd been busy all week, building a power base wherever he could. He'd gathered documentation showing that he—not Christopher—had been responsible for the development of the new memory system. He also tried to erase evidence of his shenanigans on the Atchison contract, but Matt Weed wouldn't let him get anywhere near the files.

When Bruno finished his report, Cyrus knew he still had a lot of work to do. Something had to be done before the weekend was over to convince Christopher to leave the company or drop his case. Time was running out. And even though he thought Bruno was an idiot, Cyrus knew he had to hang onto him.

"When do we get paid?" asked Bruno.

"I'll pay you when you're done," said Cyrus, "but you've got a lot more to do before you're finished. You idiots didn't do anything up there except screw around. Christopher knows why you were there and what you were trying to do. And unless he's convinced to leave the company, then we've just wasted a lot of time."

"What else do you want me and Chet to do?"

"We don't need Chet anymore," said Cyrus. "I'll give you his check and you can give it to him later. I'll know this afternoon what I want you to do."

Cyrus thought for a minute, then he asked Bruno when Christopher was supposed to come home.

"I don't know," said Bruno. "They went out to get him before we left the sheriff's office. I suppose he'll either be back tonight or tomorrow morning."

"I'll call Christopher at home tonight," said Cyrus. "If he's there, I'll find out if he's decided to stay with the company. If he has, then I'll have to think of something to do to encourage him to leave. In any event, I want you to hound him day and night. Stay on his trail and make sure he sees you. He has to think something is going to happen to him if he comes back to work, and we've got to convince him of that before Monday. If we don't, he'll start raising all sorts of hell. So, as soon as I decide what to do, I'll give you a call. In the meantime, just keep hassling him."

"Okay," said Bruno, "but when do I get paid?"

"I told you. You'll get paid when we're done. If this works out like I think it should, that will be Monday. Both you and Chet will get your money then."

Cyrus was getting to dislike Bruno more and more. He was proving to be just as big a bellyacher as his mother was. "Like mother, like son," thought Cyrus. "They're both a couple of slobs."

When Cyrus left Bruno, he told him to keep in touch. Then he went to his office to get ready for his meeting with *Mr.* Abernathy.

———

Judy talked a lot about her friendship with Lisa during the 115-mile trip from Grand Marais to Duluth. She cried openly as she told Dick about all the good times they'd had over the years. But she laughed too when she recalled some of the funny things they'd done. And some of the best times they'd ever had were in the BWCA.

Dick thought Judy was a remarkable young woman. She'd lived through two terror-filled nights and had lost her best friend. And even though she seemed to be in control of herself now, Dick knew she was in for a rough time when she got home. Close friends and family would give her support, but the loss of her best friend would be hard for her to accept. Dick thought it was a tough way to start a new life as a recent college graduate.

Then Dick thought about the tragic death of his wife. He'd been almost devastated when it happened, but the intervening years had smoothed down the rough edges. It had taken time for happy memories to replace the pain and sorrow. Dick knew it would take time for Judy too.

The more Dick listened to Judy and thought about her problems, the more sensitive he became to his own. He realized that the twenty-two year old woman sitting next to him had faced a far greater emotional upheaval than he'd faced with Bransky. His problems seemed insignificant when compared to Judy's. If Judy was able to cope with the tragic loss of her best friend, then he should be able to do as well in his dealings with Cyrus Bransky. And he shouldn't get so upset while doing it.

When they got to the Duluth airport, Dick carried Judy's bags and helped her check in for her flight to Chicago. Then he waited with her until her plane was ready to leave. When they announced her flight, she wrapped her arms around his neck and gave him a big hug. They promised to stay in touch and to see each other again. Dick knew, however, that Judy Miller would just be a part of his memory and that this would be the last time he'd ever see her. As she headed down the ramp, she turned her tear-filled eyes toward him and waved. Then she stepped inside the plane and was gone from his life forever.

144

Dick walked out of the terminal and got back into his station wagon. As he did, he felt a lump in his throat. Some very strong emotions had been stirred up by that brave young woman.

⎯

"What is it?" asked Cyrus as he picked up the intercom.

"Mr. Abernathy is here to see you, sir. He's coming right in."

Timothy Abernathy always walked right into people's offices after he'd been announced, because he liked to catch people doing things they weren't supposed to be doing. Sometimes people were caught in embarrassing situations, but Abernathy felt it was a good way to discover what was going on in the company. Especially if it was something he thought the Captain should know about.

"Good afternoon, Cyrus."

"Good afternoon, Mr. Abernathy. What can I do for you?"

"You can tell me that you and Dick Christopher have patched up your disagreements and that we won't be seeing any more problems in your area."

"I'm not sure I can do that, sir." It really irritated Cyrus to have to call this little pipsqueak, "sir".

"And why not?" demanded Abernathy.

"Mr. Christopher has been out of town all week. I haven't been able to see him, so we haven't been able to work out our differences."

"That's unfortunate, Cyrus. I was hoping I could give the Captain some good news. He's been gone these past few days too, so I don't know what kind of mood he's in. I'm going to meet with him at his lake home on Sunday, and I hope he's not going to be so upset that it spoils his weekend. He was counting on your being able to work this little problem out."

"I'll see what I can do this weekend," said Cyrus as he tried to control his temper.

"Just what *do* you plan to do, Cyrus?"

"Christopher will be home tonight or tomorrow morning. I'll call him right away and arrange a meeting. I'm sure the two of us can get our problems resolved by Monday morning."

"I certainly hope so, Cyrus. The Captain doesn't know this, but I'm aware of some fiscal irregularities that have come up in your division concerning a few selected contracts. It seems that you and some of your people have gotten yourselves into compromising situations that are not in the company's best interests. I would hate to have anything like that compound the difficulties you're having with Dick Christopher, if you know what I mean."

"Mr. Abernathy," said Cyrus, "I'll have *everything* taken care of this weekend. I can assure you of that."

"That would be nice, Cyrus. And now I've got to run. I've got a lot of work to do before I meet with the Captain. You have a nice day, Cyrus. And have a nice weekend too. I'll get back to you first thing Monday morning."

As Timothy Abernathy turned to go out the door, Cyrus gave him the finger behind his back.

Cyrus thought everyone was ganging up on him; Abernathy, Christopher, and even his bonehead nephew, Bruno. "Screw 'em all," thought Cyrus. "Especially Christopher. He's the one who got this whole mess started in the first place."

Cyrus was not about to lose his position because of Dick Christopher. If a knock-down, drag-out fight was necessary to get Christopher out of the company, then Cyrus was ready for it. He was in a battle for his survival, and he would stop at nothing to force Christopher to pull out. There had been others who had tried to take on Cyrus in the past, and he had outlasted them all. It would be the same with Christopher. Except this time the stakes were a lot higher.

Abernathy presented another problem. He apparently knew something about the skimming and payoffs with the Atchison contract. Cyrus knew Abernathy would use that information whenever it was in his best interests to do so. If Cyrus didn't get rid of Christopher by Monday, Abernathy would probably lay the whole mess in front of the Captain. That would really screw up Cyrus' position. Christopher was still the key. Cyrus could handle Abernathy when the time came, but he had to do something about Christopher right away.

Cyrus told Becky to hold his calls. Then he sat back in his chair and began to plan a foolproof method for getting Dick Christopher out of the company and out of his life. He was mad enough to do almost anything, and he was brazen enough to think he could get away with anything he tried.

Dick had lots of time to think during his three-hour drive from Duluth to Minneapolis, and he had lots to think about. He thought about the time he'd just spent in the BWCA, and he thought about the days ahead and his anticipated confrontation with Cyrus Bransky. He still couldn't decide whether he should quit the company or stay and fight. If he stayed, he knew he'd have to work very hard to pull together the information he needed for his meeting with the Captain on Monday morning.

Dick had thought spending time in the BWCA would help him come up with some answers, but it hadn't. Ellen had been right. He really went up there to escape from the problems he was having with Bransky. Now he saw escape was impossible, because the problems were still with him. As a matter of fact, the problems might have gotten worse in the time he'd been gone. Bransky could even have gained a significant advantage. Dick was suddenly aware of the fact that his procrastination had cost him a week's time and probably put him in a weaker position.

His sudden insight frustrated him. He was mad at himself for having wasted so much time. But soon his anger was replaced with determination. He didn't have much time left, but he resolved to do everything he could to get ready for Monday morning. He still didn't know if he should stay or quit the company, but he was ready to do whatever it took to come up with the right decision. At the same time, he was ready to face the consequences of his choice.

As the miles passed by, his enthusiasm grew, and soon he was confident that everything would work out to his advantage. Dick didn't know it at the time, but he would soon be faced with another crisis that could strip him of his confidence and be every bit as frightening as his adventure in the BWCA.

When Dick got to his condominium, he called Ellen and Ted and invited them for dinner. They were both ready with lots of questions, but Dick told them they'd have to wait until later. Then he put away his canoeing equipment and washed his clothes. His sleeping bag and tent were still wet, so he hung them out to dry on his balcony. Then he spent the hour he had left getting ready for dinner.

Ted and Ellen arrived within minutes of each other shortly after six. Dick kept avoiding their questions until they each had a glass of wine and were seated in the living room. Then he told them everything that happened to him from the time he'd left home. The Minneapolis paper hadn't reported anything about Lisa's killing, so neither Ted nor Ellen had heard about the episode until Dick told them. They listened with interest as Dick described his plunge in the lake and his near-fatal encounter with Lester.

"What about those two goons who came by here?" asked Ted. "Did they follow you up there?"

"Yes they did. And fortunately for me, they didn't have the vaguest notion of what they were doing." Ted and Ellen laughed when Dick told them how he marooned the two men on the island.

"After what those two tried to do to you," said Ellen, "I would expect you to raise holy hell at work on Monday."

"Wait a minute, Ellen," said Ted. "Those guys weren't just messing around. If Dick goes back to work and stirs up trouble because of what those two gorillas did, he'll get killed. I think he should quit his job and get out of there."

"Quit!" said Ellen. "He'd be crazy if he quit. He can't let that crap go on. He's got to do what's right and get Bransky fired. How can you expect him to quit? Especially now."

Dick sat back and watched his two friends go at it. He couldn't think of very many times when they were together that they didn't end up arguing about something. And yet, he knew they were both very fond of each other.

"Look, Ellen. Those guys are playing for real," said Ted. "And Cyrus Bransky has his back against the wall. You don't send two goons way up north to beat somebody's head in unless you're serious. The guy's a menace."

"That's why Dick should take him on," said Ellen. "There's already too much corruption and violence in business. Men like Bransky have to be stopped. If he can continue to bully his way around and lie and cheat and steal, then none of us is safe."

"Well that's the way it is, little lady. It's a cruel, tough world out there. And if you don't get out of the way when the trains go by, you'll get killed."

"Don't you dare patronize me," shouted Ellen. "You've been put down so much you're beginning to look like a rug. If Dick doesn't stand up for what's right, he's going to get run over just like you have. He has to fight this thing through. I just hope he doesn't listen to you."

"Bullroar!" said Ted. "Don't start giving me that crap about being stepped on. You aren't even dry behind the ears. You don't know what it's like to fight. I've been fighting all my life, and I know when it's better to walk away. Dick can't win this one. The dudes he's up against are too damn mean. He'd get killed if he listened to you."

"But it's a matter of principle," said Ellen.

"To hell with principle," said Ted. "We're talking about survival."

"Can I say something?" asked Dick.

"You stay out of this," said Ellen. "This is between me and Ted."

Dick knew better than to argue with Ellen when she had her dander up. So he backed into the kitchen and let the two of them continue their verbal assualt while he got dinner ready.

In spite of the arguing that was going on, Ted and Ellen were very sensitive people. Dick knew they could see he was having a hard time making the right decision about his job. And he knew they wanted to help. But at the same time, they still liked to argue with each other.

Ted usually stood back and chose not to get involved. He'd offer suggestions if Dick asked, but he didn't feel compelled to give advice. Now, however, he thought it was futile for Dick to challenge what he thought was an established pattern of corporate conduct. Ted felt Dick should take his lumps as they came and then quit his job and find another one.

Ellen, on the other hand, didn't hesitate at all to get actively involved in Dick's decision. She had a vested interest in what he did, because she was still thinking about marrying him. So any decision he made now could affect both of them in the future. At the same time, she saw a battle and was ready to get into it right along with Dick.

Dick wasn't ready to make a decision either way. He could see two distinct outcomes; stay and fight, or quit. These were the positions that

Ted and Ellen had taken, but other options were also available. He didn't have any trouble seeing what they were. He just didn't have a good handle on how to select among them. That was very frustrating for him, because in his job he had to deal with lots of variables. Only this time the options involved him, not a piece of computer equipment.

Dick also considered the contrast between his two friends as they debated his future. Ellen was a young woman who'd always had what she wanted. Her parents were wealthy, she'd gone to private schools, and she was never really in need. The death of her husband was a major loss that affected her emotionally, but the wealth he left was more than adequate to provide for her support. She was also a very successful stock broker who'd done extremely well on her own through lots of hard work. She was tenacious, and she wasn't about to be pushed around.

Ted was also successful, but he came from a poor black family. Athletics had given him opportunities he might never have otherwise had. He was a hard worker, but he faced the world of work like he played football. Instead of fighting when he came to a hurdle, he'd back up, look for another opening, and move in another direction. If the situation appeared hopeless or dangerous, he'd try everything he could to get away from it. He chose to fight only as a last resort.

Dick knew he'd have a hard time getting anything resolved as long as his two friends were deciding his future. As he started to get dinner ready, the phone rang.

"This is Dick Christopher," he said as he picked up the phone.

"This is Cyrus Bransky."

"Bransky? What the hell do you want?"

Ted and Ellen stopped talking and listened when they heard that Bransky was on the phone.

"I'm calling to give you some advice."

Dick could tell that Bransky had been drinking. "Okay, what advice do you have to give?"

"It would be good for your health and your future employment if you got out of the company just as fast as you can."

"Is that a threat?" asked Dick.

"You can call it anything you want. I just don't want to see you in my division anymore. I don't even want to see you anywhere. And I'll give you all the encouragement you need to find another job."

"Does that include sending your dogs after me?"

"Bruno and Chet were just trying to show you the way."

"Well the Cook County Sheriff thinks they should behave themselves and not do dumb things that can get them in trouble."

"That hick sheriff doesn't work down here," said Bransky. "And if you thought things were hairy up there, just keep screwing around down here and you'll be right back in the middle of it."

"Does the Captain know you're trying to get rid of me?"

"He's behind me one hundred percent."

Dick was sure Bransky was lying about the Captain, but he was having a hard time seeing where Bransky was coming from. If Bransky had improved his position while Dick was gone, he wouldn't have to be so aggressive. But if Bransky was in trouble, he might do just about anything to save his hide.

"Bransky," said Dick, "why don't you stop by my office on Monday and I'll tell you what I've decided to do about my job."

"If I were you," said Bransky, "I wouldn't even show up on Monday. I think you'd better get ready to move out. And the sooner the better, for your sake."

"I'd appreciate it if you and your hounds would just stay off my back. If you want to know what I'm going to do, come by Monday." With that, Dick slammed down the phone.

Neither Ted nor Ellen said anything. They sat still and watched Dick who stood for a few seconds looking at the phone. Then Dick turned to them and said, "Come on, let's get dinner on the table."

Ted and Ellen immediately started in on him, giving their suggestions on how he should handle Bransky, and at the same time arguing with each other.

"Okay," said Dick, "enough already. I'd like to have a nice quiet dinner without being harassed by Bransky or you two. Let's eat and forget about my job."

The three of them took an undeclared truce and changed the subject back to Dick's trip. While Dick cooked the steaks on the charcoal grill, Ellen finished the salad and fixed vegetables, and Ted set the table and poured the wine. After they sat down, Dick told them more about Judy and some of the things she'd gone through. Ellen was particularly interested in hearing how Judy had stood up under stress.

The evening wound down with a discussion of what Ted and Ellen had been doing for the past week. Ted finally went home about ten o'clock. By eleven o'clock Dick was showing signs of fatigue and the effects of too much wine. That's when Ellen got ready to leave.

"Hey, doll," said Dick, "why don't you stay a while and I'll fix breakfast."

"Not tonight, love. You look very tired, and I think I'd lose you in about three minutes. Get a good night's sleep and I'll come by tomorrow or Sunday. You've got a lot to think about before you go to work on Monday morning."

Dick walked with her through the hall to the lobby. Then he pulled her close and held her tight.

"Hang in there with me, Ellen. This is a hard thing for me to work out, and I don't want you to be disappointed with me."

"I may be disappointed with your decision," said Ellen, "but I'll never be disappointed with you." She gave him a long, lingering kiss. Then she stood back, smiled, and moved toward the door.

"Call me when you want to get together," she said. "We can talk. Or better yet, you can talk, and I'll listen. But just don't get your head kicked in. I sort of like your features the way they are. Good night, love."

Dick watched her go through the lobby and out the front door. Then he returned to his apartment.

He ignored the dinner dishes, went right to his bedroom, and got undressed. After a long, hot shower, he climbed into bed and turned off the light. He lay there a while, thinking about Bransky's warning and wondering what to do if Bransky tried to carry out his threats. If Bransky was going to try something, he only had two days in which to do it. But at that moment, Dick was too tired to care. Within a few minutes, he fell into a deep sleep.

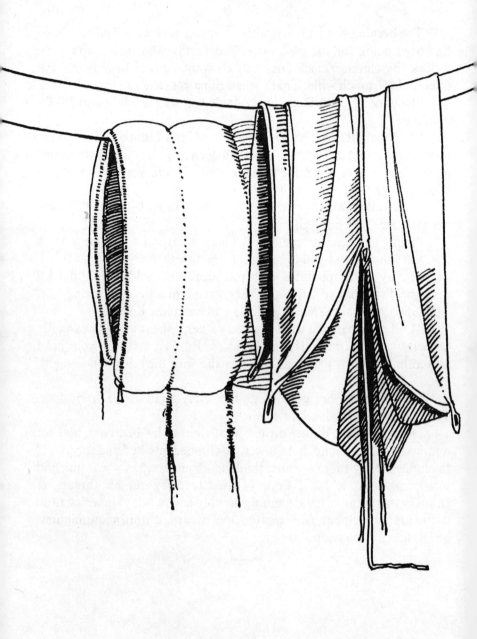

⟨⟨SATURDAY

For the first time in a long while, Dick slept in until nine o'clock. Even then he was in no hurry to get out of bed. But he knew he had to get up and take care of everything he'd neglected while he was gone. So he rolled out of bed, got dressed, fixed a big breakfast, and cleaned up the dishes he'd left the night before. He took almost an hour to clean his condominium and take care of the mail that had come.

He thought about his relationship with Bransky while he was doing his housekeeping tasks. The call he got last night had added to his enthusiasm for finding a quick solution. So when he was all done cleaning, he found some notepaper and started writing things down. The first thing he did was develop a balance sheet of reasons why he should quit or stay with the company. He put all the reasons for staying on one half of the page and all the reasons for leaving on the other half. He'd write something down, and then he'd go back to doing household chores. Whenever he got another idea, he'd stop what he was doing and write it down. This meant a lot of going back and forth, but he was finally starting to pull things together to the point where he could make a decision.

At one-thirty he decided to go to the supermarket for groceries. He drove out of the garage, through the parking lot, and into the street. Suddenly, a black van cut across in front of him and forced him to the curb. He killed his engine when he slammed on the brakes, and then he immediately tried to get it started again. The van made a U-turn in the middle of the street and pulled up right next to him. The driver's window rolled down and Bruno stuck his head out.

"Why don't you watch where you're going, Christopher?"

153

"What the hell do you want?" asked Dick.

"I just wanted to tell you that Uncle Cyrus is really serious about your leaving his company."

"*His* company?"

"Yeah," said Bruno, "his company. He thinks you'd be a lot better off working somewhere else. He'd be happier too. So why don't you wise up and take a hint. You're not wanted."

"Why don't you go find a canoe and get lost?" said Dick.

"Don't get smart with me," said Bruno. "I still owe you for the fun and games you pulled up north. I could bust your head in just for the hell of it."

"What do you want?" asked Dick.

"Just do like you're told," said Bruno. "Leave Uncle Cyrus alone and go and find yourself another job."

"I'll think about it," said Dick as he turned to start his engine again.

"Yeah, you think about it," said Bruno. "Because if you're still around on Monday, we'll be back with some stronger words of encouragement."

Dick started his station wagon and pulled back from the curb. Then, without looking at Bruno, he continued straight ahead down the street. In the rearview mirror he saw Bruno make another U-turn and fall in behind him.

Dick turned down a side street and cut over to the main boulevard that led to the shopping center. He took a roundabout way of going to the grocery store to see if Bruno would follow him. The van stayed behind him all the way. That made it clear to Dick that Bruno would be with him for quite a while. Or at least until Monday.

Dick parked in the grocery store lot, went in, and did his shopping. When he came back out thirty minutes later, Bruno was still waiting in his van at the edge of the parking lot. Dick made three more stops on other errands and Bruno stayed with him all the time. When Dick went back to his condominium, Bruno followed him home. As Dick drove into his garage, he looked back and saw Bruno park his van across the street from the parking lot.

Dick went upstairs to his apartment, put away his groceries, and cleaned up the kitchen. Then he sat down with his notepad and began to write out a plan of action. The more he wrote, the harder it got for him to decide what to do. He found he had just as many good reasons for staying as for leaving. In either case, he felt he had to have an early Monday morning meeting with Bransky and the Captain. Then he'd lay everything on the table and announce what he was going to do. But the meeting had to be set up right away, and the person to do that was Bransky's secretary, Becky Richards. Dick called her at home.

"Hello, doll. This is Dick Christopher."

"Well hello, stranger. I'm glad you're back. I hear you had quite a week up north."

"I'll tell you about it sometime, but now I'd like you to do me a favor. Try to get ahold of Abernathy and tell him I'd like to schedule a meeting with the Captain and Cyrus Bransky for nine o'clock Monday morning. Tell him it's very important."

"Are you declaring war?" asked Becky.

"Almost," said Dick. "I'll have to see if anybody else is going to fight."

"Well we're way ahead of you, dear. I used to think Saturday was my day off, but not today. Abernathy already called me and told me to set up the same meeting. He also wants to get together at nine. I just called Bransky and was getting ready to call you. I get the feeling that lots of things are starting to happen, but I don't know what they are."

"You'll know when I do," said Dick. "It's probably a war council. If the Captain called it, he must have some idea of what's going on. I'm anxious to hear what he has to say, but don't look for me before nine."

"Okay, dear. We'll see you then. Good luck."

"Thanks, Becky. I'll need it."

After Dick hung up, he unplugged both of his telephones so no one would bother him. Then he went back to the analysis he was making about his job. He got out the documentation he'd gathered during the development of the memory-system project and spread it out on his dining room table. He worked all afternoon on his plan, but no matter what he did, he was no closer to a decision about staying or leaving.

In spite of Dick's frustration, he did accomplish several things. He had a better idea of what his options were, and he knew what data he had to have before he went to the Captain. He also knew how he would handle the information Matt Weed had. So even though he didn't know

156

what decision he'd make, he at least felt he'd be able to come up with a workable solution. He was getting his confidence back, feeling more at ease, and starting to look forward to his Monday morning meeting. On the other hand, Cyrus Bransky was feeling entirely different about the situation.

———

Cyrus Bransky was very upset when Becky Richards told him the Captain had called a nine o'clock meeting for Monday morning. Cyrus knew what would happen at that meeting. Christopher and Abernathy would tell the Captain all about Cyrus' pirating and skimming. And if the Captain didn't like what he heard, he'd probably decide to fire Cyrus.

Cyrus felt trapped. He knew he had to take some drastic action to save his job and keep his world from crashing down on top of him.

Cyrus still felt Christopher was the cause of all his problems, and the only way he could save his job was to get Christopher out of the company once and for all. He wanted to kill him, but he didn't think he could get away with it unless he either made it look like an accident or steered the blame onto someone else.

Everybody knew Cyrus was mad at Christopher. But Cyrus wondered about the people down in Chicago who got their drug ring busted up. He figured somebody there must hate Christopher just as much as he did.

Cyrus didn't think people would get too upset if he did something to hurt Christopher without killing him. If anyone asked him about it, he'd say he had nothing to do with it. He'd just tell whoever was interested that the people in Chicago had a lot more reasons to get Christopher than he did. Cyrus knew one thing for sure. He had to get the job done before the Monday morning meeting with the Captain.

Cyrus sat back then and thought of all the things he'd like to do to Christopher. Then he remembered his friend who ran an auto body shop over in Arden Hills. The man was a nut about war and weapons and had invented all kinds of devices for destroying or disabling anything that walked. He managed to stay just ahead of the law by saying it was a hobby and he never used any of his inventions except to get rid of pests and vermin that hung around his shop. But his inventions did disappear on occasion, which made Cyrus think he was selling them. Cyrus hadn't seen his friend for several months, but he definitely remembered some of his inventions. One in particular stood out in Cyrus' mind. The more he thought about it, the more he liked the idea of using it on Christopher. He decided then to visit his friend early Sunday afternoon to see if he still had what Cyrus was looking for. Hopefully he did, because Cyrus felt it was something Dick Christopher would really get a bang out of.

⚓SUNDAY

Dick Christopher got up early, ate a big breakfast, read the morning paper, and went for a walk. When he got outside, he noticed that Bruno had not yet taken up his position across the street. He knew, however, that before the day was over, Bruno's black van would be back in its customary position.

When Dick got back to his apartment, he went right to work on his problem with Bransky. He was still trying to decide if he should stay or quit, but he was a lot closer to making a decision now than he'd ever been before. With all the information he'd accumulated, he felt he could be comfortable with either choice. And he knew he'd shake up some people in the company regardless of the one he chose. Now he was looking for the key. Something that would tip the balance so dramatically that it would have a significant impact on everyone who would be affected by it.

At ten o'clock, Dick took a break and went to the drug store. He no sooner was out of his garage when Bruno's van pulled up behind him. Bruno tailgated him, honked his horn several times, and generally made a pest out of himself. As soon as Dick got home, Bruno called him on the intercom from the lobby.

"What do you want?" demanded Dick.

"I just wanted you to know that we're still thinking about you," said Bruno.

Dick hung up the intercom and went back to work. Bransky's goons hadn't laid a hand on him yet, and he was beginning to think they weren't going to. If they continued to do the same dumb things, he didn't think he'd have much to worry about.

But Dick was being a little overconfident. Because at that moment, Cyrus Bransky was making his move to scuttle Dick once and for all.

—

Cyrus drove over to his friend's body shop around one o'clock Sunday afternoon. He parked in the front lot and walked around to the living quarters in the rear. Ozzie Simmons was lying in a hammock in the backyard, drinking beer and watching the Twins baseball game on TV. He got up when he saw Cyrus.

"Cyrus, old buddy. How the hell are you?"

"Fine, Ozzie. How are you?"

"Just great. The Twins might even win one today. What brings you out here on such a nice day?"

"I'm here on business, Ozzie. I'd like to talk to you about that invention you showed me last time I was out. I think you called it the 'octupus'."

Ozzic's eyes brightened. He always liked to show off his inventions, especially if he thought he might be able to sell one. He and Cyrus walked into the rear of the body shop and over to a large metal cabinet. Ozzie unlocked it and took out a box. He carried the box to a nearby worktable and opened it.

"Here it is, Cyrus. Don't it look pretty?"

"Show me again how it works," said Cyrus.

"Okay. First you disconnect the speedometer cable from the transmission housing. Then you attach this little magneto device to the cable and hook it back up again. It's simple. Right?

"Then you take these five wires that come off the magneto and you attach these little clips to each one. You take four of these clips and put one on each of the four brake lines, up next to the wheel. You attach the fifth clip to one of the lube joints on the tie rod. Okay? You got that?"

"Does each clip have to be placed in an exact spot?" asked Cyrus.

"No," said Ozzie. "That's what's so beautiful about it. Just so four of the clips are on the brake lines and the other one is on a lube joint. It'll fit any car.

"Now, you take these little plastic wads of dynamite and attach one to each clip. The big one goes on the lube joint."

"Then what happens?" asked Cyrus.

"When the car gets going about fifty or fifty-five miles an hour, the magneto sends a spark to each clip. Then—kaboom! The dynamite blows. Nothing big, hardly any noise at all. But all four brake lines will split, and the tie rod should break. Whoever is driving the car is going to have a helluva time trying to stop without running into something."

"Is this the only one you've got?" asked Cyrus.

"Yeah. Why? Do you want to buy it?"

"Yes I do," said Cyrus. "How much do you want for it?"

"Well I'll be damned, Cyrus. I didn't think you had it in you. Sure, I'll sell it to you. And since you're a good friend, it'll only cost you five hundred bucks."

"Okay," said Cyrus, "I'll take it. Can I give you a check?"

"Nope," said Ozzie. "I don't want no checks. Just cash."

"I don't have that much with me right now," said Cyrus. "Can I bring the cash by tomorrow after I've used it?"

"Sure. Why not? I trust you, Cyrus. And besides, if you used it and didn't pay for it, I'd have to tell the cops you stole it from me. And you wouldn't want me to do that, would you?"

"I'll bring you the cash just as soon as I go to the bank."

"Who are you going to use it on?" asked Ozzie.

"A man that works for me. I'm having a hard time communicating with him."

"Well you use this little gadget, Cyrus, and I'll guarantee you he'll get the message."

"Yes," thought Cyrus. "He'll get the message. Loud and clear."

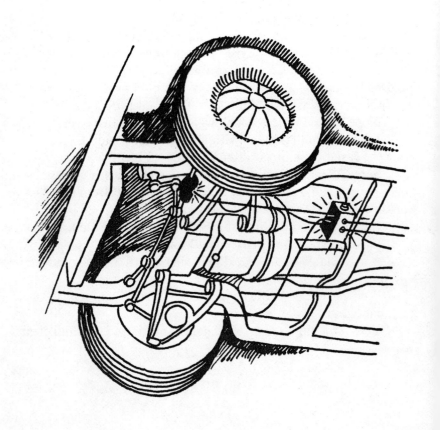

☙ MONDAY

Cyrus Bransky got out of bed at four o'clock. He was so excited about what he was going to do that he went right to his car without getting anything to eat. He opened his trunk and looked again at the explosive device he'd picked up from Ozzie Simmons. If Christopher was dumb enough to drive to work this morning, then he'd miss his meeting with the Captain. Because somewhere along the highway, Dick Christopher was going to be in one helluva car accident. Cyrus smiled broadly as he closed the trunk and got into his car. He could hardly wait to put his scheme into action.

Cyrus drove to Bruno's apartment, went to the door, and knocked several times before Bruno answered.

"What the hell have you been doing?" yelled Cyrus. "I told you when I called last night that I'd be here early."

"But goddamnit," wailed Bruno, "it's only four-thirty."

"Get dressed," snapped Cyrus. "We've got to go right now. I'll go down and wait for you by your van. Get going!"

Bruno quickly got dressed. He still didn't know what his uncle was up to, but he knew it involved Christopher. He was dressed and outside in less than ten minutes.

"What took you so goddamn long?" demanded Cyrus who was getting to be a nervous wreck.

"Hey, calm down, Uncle Cyrus. I'm here, ain't I?"

"We've got to take your van. I don't want anyone to see me in my car."

"Thanks a lot," said Bruno. "Then if we get into some kind of trouble, I'll get the blame."

"Don't worry about it," said Cyrus. "Just get in." Cyrus went over to his car, got the explosive device out of his trunk, and set it in Bruno's van.

"What did you put in there?" asked Bruno.

Cyrus described the device and told Bruno how it worked.

"As soon as Christopher reaches fifty or fifty-five miles an hour, each of the charges will blow. The little ones will sever the brake lines, and the big one will pop the tie rod."

"Then what happens?" asked Bruno.

"We'll see how good a driver our friend Dick Christopher is. He won't have any brakes, and he won't be able to steer. But I'm sure he'll manage to stop somehow. Actually, I expect him to smash the hell out of his car."

"But he could get killed," said Bruno.

"Maybe so," said Cyrus, "or maybe not. But one thing's certain, he's going to get the crap scared out of him. And he won't be coming to work today. Or any day for the next week if this thing works the way it's supposed to."

"Uncle Cy, I think you're crazy."

━

Bruno drove into the parking lot at Dick's condominium and parked his van in the far corner, near the service door that led to the garage.

"I want you to go in there and hook this thing up," said Cyrus. "It's very simple, and it shouldn't take you very long to do. I'll stand guard outside the door so nobody bothers us."

Cyrus showed Bruno how to connect the device to Dick's car. When Bruno said he understood what to do, they got out of the van and headed for the garage. Bruno opened the door with one of his security keys and went inside with the explosive device, a tool box, and a flashlight. Cyrus stayed outside and kept watch. It was less than an hour before sunrise.

While Bruno was working on Dick's station wagon, Cyrus was nervously pacing back and forth in front of the door. He stopped suddenly when he heard a noise on the hill in back of the garage. He looked up and saw four large dogs running through the trees. There wasn't enough light to identify them clearly, but Cyrus thought he saw two German shepards, an Irish setter, and a black labrador. When the dogs got to the crest of the hill, they stopped and looked down at Cyrus who was only fifty yards away from them. Cyrus saw the dogs and stood very still.

Then one of the German shepards started to growl. That was enough for Cyrus. He opened the service door and yelled in at Bruno to hurry up and finish. Then he started to move very slowly toward the van, which was about twenty yards away.

As soon as the dogs saw Cyrus move, they followed him very closely with their eyes. Then two more dogs started to growl. That made Cyrus move a little faster. But as soon as he did, the dogs started running down the hill right at him. When Cyrus saw them coming, he started to run as fast as he could for the van. He was absolutely terrified, because he was scared to death of dogs.

A commotion outside Dick's building woke him about five o'clock. He bounded out of bed, showered, shaved, and got dressed. Then he fixed a big breakfast of eggs, bacon, hashbrowns, and toast. He was excited over the prospect of a very eventful day.

He had several cups of coffee as he watched the morning news on TV. When the morning paper arrived, he took his time reading it. Then he got out his notes again and reassessed his options. He felt good, and he felt ready for his upcoming meeting with Bransky and the Captain. At the same time, he was aware of some of the future problems his decision would bring.

He loaded his dishes in the dishwasher and laughed to himself when he thought about this being his last meal. He was confident that he'd made the right decision, but he also knew he could be in for some real trouble before the day was over.

Dick usually left for work at seven o'clock. He always took the interstate across town and got to his office at seven-thirty. That gave him an hour of solitude before everyone else came in at eight-thirty. But today he wanted to delay his departure. He planned to leave at eight-twenty and arrive at nine, just in time for his scheduled meeting with Bransky and the Captain. The traffic on the interstate would be a lot heavier, but he wanted to avoid contact with his co-workers before he went into his meeting. He was emotionally and intellectually ready, and he didn't want anyone to sidetrack him.

He enjoyed his early morning leisure. He watched the "TODAY" show for the first time in months. He went over his notes. He reread the morning paper. He even stood in front of the mirror in his bedroom and rehearsed what he planned to say. Then it was time to go.

At eight-twenty he made sure everything was turned off in the apartment. Then he got his Volvo keys and started for the door.

He was out in the hall, ready to close the door, when he remembered his tapes of conversations he'd had with Bransky. He'd set aside four that he thought were critical to the defense of his position. When he went back inside to get them, he noticed that the phones were still unplugged. He didn't want to leave anything in disarray, so he plugged them back in.

He'd no sooner plugged in the phone in the kitchen when it rang. It was Becky Richards.

"Dick, I've tried to contact you for the past half hour."

"The phone was disconnected. What's up?"

"Something terrible has happened. Mr. Bransky and his nephew were walking in a park somewhere in south Minneapolis when they were attacked by several dogs. Mr. Bransky apparently got real scared and his nephew thought he'd had a heart attack. He put him in his van and drove to Fairview Hospital, but he was too late. Mr. Bransky is dead."

"Dead! Holy cow!"

Dick was stunned. It wasn't that he cared that much for Cyrus. He didn't. But a sudden death always bothered him, especially when it involved someone he knew. And this was one more death to add to the two he'd just faced on the Gunflint Trail.

Dick's mind raced over the events of the past week, including the preparations he'd made for this morning's meeting with Bransky and the Captain. Becky's voice brought him back to the immediate problem.

"You'd better get over here as soon as you can, Dick. As far as I know, you're still supposed to meet with the Captain. But you're supposed to see Matt Weed first. Now I've got to let you go, because I've got a ton of work to do. I'll see you when you get here."

After Becky hung up, Dick stood by the phone for a moment and tried to figure out what was going to happen next. He knew this was going to be a wild day when he got out of bed, but he didn't expect it to start off like this. He looked around his apartment again to make sure everything was in order. Then he closed the door behind him and headed for work.

Dick hurried down to the garage and got in his station wagon. He knew he'd better not waste any time if the Captain and Matt Weed were waiting for him. He drove through the garage to the overhead door and pressed his automatic opener. Nothing happened. Then he saw the note on the door.

"Out of order. Please open by hand." The note had been signed by the caretaker.

Dick raised the door and hurried back to his station wagon. But before he could get back in, the door fell shut with a bang. He turned around, swore at the door, and raised it again. He held it for a few seconds to make sure it would stay open, then he hurried back to his wagon and drove through. He stopped again outside, got out, and went back to close the door. He gave it a little push for good measure, and when it hit the garage floor, it almost came off its runners.

Dick could already feel stress building inside him. Bransky's death had deeply affected him, and now he started worrying about his impending meeting with Matt Weed and the Captain. He knew he'd better calm down, because if he let little things like a broken garage door get to him, he'd be in real trouble before the day was over.

He drove to the street, turned left, and headed toward Interstate 35. As he picked up speed, he turned on the radio to hear the traffic report. It didn't sound good. I-35 was very busy for Monday morning with lots of stop-and-go traffic all the way into downtown Minneapolis. He decided instead to take Highway 100 north to Highway 12. He could go east on 12, catch I-35 outside the loop, and hopefully miss a lot of the inbound traffic.

Highway 100 was almost as bad as I-35. Traffic was slowed down all the way to the crosstown highway. Everytime Dick thought he had an opening where he could speed up, someone cut him off. His frustration with the traffic reminded him of why he usually drove to work much earlier. He wasn't used to heavy traffic and it bothered him. No matter what he did to speed up, he stayed confined to a snail-like pace.

Dick didn't know it, but Cyrus' little explosive device was operating the way it was supposed to. The magneto was still attached to the transmission housing and the wires were all connected to other parts of the vehicle. The magneto rotor was spinning right along in sync with the speedomoter cable. The faster Dick went, the faster went the rotor. But so far, Dick had not approached the speed that would set off the explosives.

When Dick got through the stoplight at Thirty-sixth Avenue, he saw a clear lane ahead and stepped down hard on the accelerator. His speed climbed rapidly to fifty miles an hour. Then, with no warning at all, a car came down the ramp from his right, cut across the outside lane, and pulled right in front of him. He hit the brakes and the horn at the same time and narrowly avoided a rear-end collision. The young woman who cut in front of Dick looked back at him in her rear-view mirror and gave him the finger.

By now, Dick was really getting upset. But there was absolutely nothing he could do about it except move with the rest of the traffic. When he got to the off-ramp to Highway 12, traffic had slowed to a crawl. He found himself right behind a delivery truck and began inhaling its obnoxious exhaust fumes. He closed his fresh-air vent and started to sweat.

"Damnit," he said aloud. "I should have stayed up north."

His mind wandered back to the lakes and streams of the Boundary Waters Canoe Area. He thought of the clear, crisp morning air and the smell of pine trees and compared it to the noise and stench that was right in front of him. He finally accepted the fact that he couldn't do anything about the traffic except move with it like everybody else. So he eased back in his seat, thought about being up north, and started to relax. He even managed to smile at the other drivers as they plodded along next to him.

As soon as Dick got through the Lowry tunnel and on to north-bound I-35, the traffic started to thin out. He was able to accelerate up to fifty miles an hour as he crossed the Mississippi River past the University of Minnesota. The little magneto rotor accelerated right along with him toward the point where it was supposed to set off the explosives.

Dick was driving in the far left lane, next to the divider. To his right, one car length back, was a big 18-wheeler with a full load of grain. As far as Dick was concerned, the big truck was too close for comfort. He had to get off the interstate in a mile and a half, so he knew he'd have to accelerate ahead of the truck and cut across in front of it before he got to the exit. He couldn't drop back behind the truck because there were too many cars back there.

He moved his turn signal up for a right turn and stepped down on the accelerator pedal. He didn't gain an inch on the truck, so he pushed the pedal all the way to the floor. He sure didn't want to get caught in front of the truck when he had to slow down for the exit. And if he had to make a quick stop, he was afraid the truck would run right over the top of him.

Dick looked again in his outside rearview mirror and then cut right in front of the big semi. He was now going close to sixty and the truck was less than ten feet behind him. The rotor in the magneto was spinning wildly, keeping pace with the speedometer cable that drove it.

Right then Dick heard a loud chirping noise coming up from the transmission housing. That was followed immediately by a clicking noise from behind his dashboard.

"Damn," he thought, "my speedometer cable is going out on me."

He looked at the speedometer and saw the needle waving back and forth between 0 and 90 miles an hour.

Now the truck was right on Dick's tail, waiting for him to make his move, but not backing off an inch. The exit was just ahead. He checked his mirror again, saw that the outside lane was clear, and signaled to move right. The accelerator was on the floor, and the chirping and grinding noises were getting louder. Dick swung the wheel quickly to the right and headed down the exit ramp. The big truck zoomed past him with inches to spare.

Dick came to a stop at the end of the ramp, turned right, and headed for the company complex. As he picked up speed, the noises started up again, only louder. To save time, and because he was in a hurry, Dick decided to park in the circular drive in front of the administration building. It was a designated no-parking zone, but it was a lot closer than the employees' lot.

Dick left his station wagon and went right to Matt Weed's office. Matt got up to greet him as he walked in the door.

"Dick, it's good to see you," said Matt. "I hear you had quite a week."

"Things have been wild all over," said Dick. "I got a call this morning about Cyrus Bransky."

"As much as I disliked him, it was still a tough way to go," said Matt. "But if he hadn't gone on his own, I think the Captain would have done him in."

"Why do you say that?" asked Dick.

"Last Saturday the Captain paid a surprise visit to his office. As you know, he never works on the weekend. It was probably the first time he was in on a Saturday morning in his life. A good client had given him a new putter, and he'd forgotten to take it home. On Friday night the client called and invited him to play a round of golf Saturday afternoon at the Minneapolis Golf Club. The Captain knew he couldn't show up without his new putter, so he came into the office to get it. When he got there, he found Timothy Abernathy going through his files. The Captain had just been talking to Abernathy before he came down to the office."

"What was Abernathy doing there?" asked Dick. "He never works weekends either."

"Apparently he did," said Matt. "At least he did whenever he wanted to go through the Captain's files. He was building a case against Cyrus and was digging up everything he could get his hands on. When the Captain walked into his office, he found Abernathy with his dirty linen spread all over the desk."

"What happened then?" asked Dick.

"First of all, the Captain was mad because Abernathy was in his files. Then he started going through the stuff Abernathy had laid out and saw what Bransky had been involved in. The Captain really got mad when he realized that Abernathy knew all about the skimming and payoffs but had never told him about it. The Captain also figured out that Abernathy was going to use the information to blackmail Bransky.

"Fortunately for Abernathy, the security guard had seen the Captain go into the building and had followed him to see if something was wrong. If the guard hadn't come in the office when he did, the Captain might have clobbered Abernathy on the head with his putter."

"What did he do to Abernathy?"

"The Captain fired him on the spot. He told the guard to take Abernathy's keys and throw him out of the building. Then before he left for his golf game, the Captain took another look at the stuff Abernathy had gathered and called me. He told me to get right over there, find out what I could about what was going on, and report to him at his home on Sunday morning."

"Did you?"

"Yes I did. Most of what was there I already knew about, but never had proof of. I'll give Abernathy credit, he did a heck of a job getting it all together."

"What did the Captain say when you reported to him?"

"He wanted Bransky's head right then. He tried to call him several times on Sunday but could never reach him. He knew Cyrus would be in this morning for the nine o'clock meeting, so he decided to fire him then."

"Does the Captain still want to see me?"

"Yes, definitely. But of course the whole situation is much different now. The Captain knows how Bransky used you for the past couple of years. He also knows that you've been doing some real good things. So he's decided to put you in Bransky's old job. As of today, you're vice president in charge of the entire research division."

Dick was elated. He felt he'd finally gotten his just reward for several years of hard work. He still felt bad about Bransky's death, but he wasn't going to let it dampen his enthusiasm. He was also happy to see that Abernatry had been given the axe. Things were starting to look up for Dick.

His jubilation was interrupted, however, by a call on Matt's intercom.

"Dick," said Matt after he hung up his phone, "that was Security calling. Your station wagon is illegally parked in front of the building. They're going to tow it if you don't get it back to the employee's lot right away. Why don't you take care of it now. Then stop by your office if you have to. I'll tell the Captain you're here. We should be getting together in his office in about twenty minutes."

Dick thanked Matt and hurried out to his station wagon. As he got in, he saluted the security guard who was waiting in a patrol car behind him.

Dick pulled away from the curb, and the noise started up again. He didn't want to take the time to find out what it was, so he tried to ignore it. He turned back on Stinson Boulevard and headed quickly for the parking lot. Just as he wheeled into an empty parking space, all hell broke loose.

Bang! Pow! Pow! Pow! Pow!

Dick's hood flew open and all four wheel covers popped off onto the pavement. A cloud of black smoke swept over the entire station wagon.

The noise was no more than that of four firecrackers and a shotgun blast, but it scared the daylights out of Dick. The security guard who had been following behind dashed out of his car with a fire extinguisher in hand. He sprayed everything he could, including most of Dick. The two of them looked over the entire vehicle but couldn't see anything wrong. There had been no fire, and there seemed to be no structural damage. Then the guard crawled underneath and spotted the five loose wires and the magneto. He crawled back out and told Dick what he'd found.

"It looks like someone was trying to do you in, Mr. Christopher. I think you've been bombed, but they sure did a lousy job of it. No offense intended, sir. It's just that whoever did it got all the wires screwed up."

"Bransky," thought Dick. "It must have been him and that neanderthal nephew of his."

"I'll check it over for you, sir. And I'll let you know if there's anything wrong. Otherwise it just looks like you might need some new wheel covers."

Dick thanked the guard, gathered up his briefcase and tapes, and headed for his meeting with the Captain. He hoped the rest of the day would be a lot quieter than it had been so far. Once again he thought about the peace and quiet of the Boundary Waters Canoe Area. As he headed down the corridor toward his office, he was already thinking about another—but hopefully a less adventurous—canoe trip. Next time, however, he wouldn't go to the Gunflint to escape his responsibilities. He'd face his detractors, resolve his difficulties, complete his tasks, and then submerge himself in the glory of the wilderness.

When Dick opened the double doors to the research division, he was greeted by the applause of his entire staff. In spite of a somewhat lousy week, Dick Christopher was happy to be back.

THE END

ORDER FORM

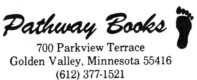